STEAMY SHORTS 5

A Collection of Steampunk, Science Fiction
and other Erotic Short Stories

By
Jean Ecrivain

Copyright & Legal

© 2017, All rights reserved
Cover designed by Lisa Gravelle-Ford,
http://www.dragonportraits.com
© 2017 used with permission

ISBN: 978-1976423871

THIS IS A WORK OF FICTION. All characters, events, and locations are the product of the writer's imagination. Any resemblance to any person living or dead or any location or other is purely coincidence. And completely unbelievable.

The activities depicted in this book are intended for the entertainment of adults. If you are below the age of majority in your jurisdiction, PLEASE STOP READING. The author and/or publisher and/or bookseller is not responsible for the purchase or use of this book in jurisdictions where depiction of adult relationship activities is forbidden. If you are in such a jurisdiction, PLEASE STOP READING. The activities depicted in this book may or may not be harmful, dangerous, or even impossible. In any case, they should not be attempted in real life. In real life always practice safe, sane, and consensual sex.

R20171002.075400

**For my Toy
You're my
private breeding stud.**

Other Books by Jean Ecrivain

On Kindle:
A Taste for the Night Series
A Taste for the Night Book 1 Arrival
A Taste for the Night Book 2 Settling In

Chasing Fae Romance Series
Book 1 Well Met in Forest Light
Book 2 Well Met in Castle Light
Book 3 Well Met in Dragon Light (coming Nov/2017)

Steamy Shorts
Steamy Shorts 1
Steamy Shorts 2
Steamy Shorts 3
Steamy Shorts 4
Steamy Shorts 5

In Print:
A Taste for the Night Series
A Taste for the Night Book 2 Settling In
(includes Bonus of Book 1)

Chasing Fae Romance Series
Book 1 Well Met in Forest Light
Book 2 Well Met in Castle Light
Book 3 Well Met in Dragon Light (coming Nov/2017)

Steamy Shorts
Steamy Shorts 1
Steamy Shorts 2
Steamy Shorts 3
Steamy Shorts 4
Steamy Shorts 5

Would you like a free book?

or maybe two or three?
Want to know when my next book is coming out?
Want a chance to read my books in advance?

Then sign up for my newsletter ...

https://jeanecrivain.wordpress.com/newsletter/

Table of Contents

INTRODUCTION	**1**
A NOTE FROM THE AUTHOR	5
1. THE ENGINE ROOM	**9**
PREFACE	9
THE ENGINE ROOM	11
2. STEAMY KNICKERS	**37**
PREFACE	37
STEAMY KNICKERS	39
3. NOT YOUR TYPICAL EARWORM	**69**
PREFACE	69
NOT YOUR TYPICAL EARWORM	71
4. THE SEX CODER	**95**
PREFACE	95
THE SEX CODER	97
5. THE BARN	**119**
PREFACE	119
THE BARN	123
NOTES FROM THE AUTHOR	**147**
A NOTE FROM THE AUTHOR	147
ABOUT THE AUTHOR	149
OTHER BOOKS BY JEAN ECRIVAIN	**151**
SAMPLES	**152**
THE BARN	153
A TASTE FOR THE NIGHT BOOK 1 ARRIVAL	159
A TASTE FOR THE NIGHT BOOK 2 SETTLING IN	167
CHASING FAE ROMANCE BOOK 1 WELL MET IN FOREST LIGHT	181

CHASING FAE ROMANCE BOOK 2 WELL MET IN CASTLE LIGHT	189
CHASING FAE ROMANCE BOOK 3 WELL MET IN DRAGON LIGHT	207
THE STEAMY SHORTS SERIES	221

Introduction

Welcome to the fifth book in my Steamy Shorts series.

I am expecting this to be the last of this series of books. If it actually will be or not is something that only the future can tell for sure. When I started, I figured that I might produce three books or maybe at the outside four books in the series. Oops. I've hit five and I'm thinking of starting even more series like this. Let's just say that I've enjoyed writing this series much more than I had expected to.

When I wrote the first book in this series, I did so for several reasons.

First, I had a backlog of short stories that I had written for a number of reasons. Since I always begin my full-length books by writing the first chapter as a short story, I had a number of short stories that had never seen the light of day. Or more correctly a reading light. This was a way for me to put those stories out.

Secondly, it was a way for me to produce new books quickly. A novel takes a long time to write. Even at my maximum output, I can't produce one in less than a month. And then comes the actual editing, and publication process. Of course, life happens and I don't ever produce at maximum output for long periods. So typically, writing a novel will take me six months or more. Short stories, on the other hand, run one to two days for me to write. So I can produce four short stories in one to two weeks if life agrees. And they make nice breaks between books.

Third, it was a way for me to produce and sell books cheaply. By selling books cheaply, I introduce new readers to my books and with luck, they'll like my writing enough to buy my other books.

Thus this series was born.

In this series, you'll find everything I'm interested in. From space opera to steampunk, from urban fantasy to historical-that-never-was romance. The only unifying thread is that the characters love sex in all its myriad forms. And they enjoy being characters in an Erotic novel.

Introduction

Of course, things haven't quite worked out the way I expected when I started this series. Amongst other things, I found that I was writing Erotica stories outside of Steampunk, Science Fiction, and Fantasy. But I didn't have anywhere to publish those stories. And while it's been a pleasure writing S/SF/F stories, I'd like to try other types of erotica from time to time.

Plus Steamy Shorts went on rather longer than I expected or is economic. I expected 3 books plus a compendium. I've got five, which means the compendium is quite a bit larger than is practical. Also the cost of production (in terms of writing time) has been somewhat higher than expected. This meant that using this series as a loss-leader hasn't worked out quite the way I wanted.

While Steamy Shorts may be ending, I'm not finished writing short stories. Look out for my other collections. I may even do another collection of SFF Erotica. We shall see.

And of course, I do write novel length books which I would love for you to try.

I hope you'll enjoy reading about my stories as much as I enjoy writing them. And if we each have half as much fun as my characters have living their Erotica stories, then we should both be very satisfied.

By the way, if there is a particular story you would like to see as a book, or a particular scene you would like portrayed in a future short story, please let me know. You can contact me via Facebook at https://www.facebook.com/jean.ecrivain or send me an email at jeanecrivain@gmail.com or use the contact me page at http://jeanecrivain.wordpress.com.

Jean E.

Ontario, Canada

A note from the author

Most writers enjoy spreading their wings. Most writers also depend on their readers for inspiration. This book is an extreme example of those two characteristics.

Because these are short stories, I can take chances. I can write stories that go beyond my rather perverted (and. so I'm learning, rather limited) interests and fantasies.

But to do that I need your help.

First, if there is anything you would like me to write about – situation, theme, sex act, characters – anything at all, please ask. That's all it will take.

You can contact me (and follow me) through any of: my Facebook page which can be found at https://www.facebook.com/jean.ecrivain or through my

Amazon author's page which can be found at http://www.amazon.com/author/jeanecrivain or via good old email at jeanecrivain@gmail.com, or through my website at http://jeanecrivain.wordpress.com. Of course, you can also find me on one of the many Facebook groups I hang out in. I do respond to everyone and I really do want your opinions. So come along and say hello.

Secondly, you can help by reviewing this (and my other books). By reviewing the books you read, you'll help other readers to spot the books that are worth reading and bypass the ones that aren't.

Jean E.
Ontario, Canada

1. The Engine Room

Preface

Tentacle Hentai sometimes seems to be the most common form of Japanese porn. This story was written about the same time as "The Collection" in Steamy Shorts 4 was written. And it came out of the same flipping through videos with Toy session as "The Collection". Of course, along with all the other kinks and blowjobs there was a lot of tentacle porn being flipped though. And some being watched, of course.

I've always wanted to write tentacle porn but frankly, it was something that I didn't understand. Let's face it, tentacle porn is just plain strange at the best of times. Getting a penis substitute stuck in one's ear or up one's nose just doesn't do it for me.

But during this particular movie night there were two scenes that seemed to stick with me. One was a standard Bimbos in Space movie. Actually, it was Dominatrixes in Space as I recall. Not that there was much difference in the case of this movie. Pretty standard Science Fiction erotica all in all and not particularly memorable. But the airlock interested me for some strange reason. Maybe because it was the only scenery in the movie. Maybe because it actually was futuristic. What can I say, there are times I'm a little strange.

After we'd flipped past that video, there was a Tentacle Hentai video. It was about as memorable as the Science Fiction movie, in fact. But it had one scene where the heroine is smothered in tentacles. She's in the middle of the moving mass of tentacles and slowly disappears as they swarm her.

After those two movies, I took over the mouse and Toy watched what I chose.

The next morning, "The Collection" sprang out of my overactive imagination. Followed immediately by this story and Not Your Typical Earworm. Three stories from the same inspiration. And I got to use a different version of my name in one of my stories. Wow, maybe I'll be famous! You can't beat that for value.

Enjoy!

The Engine Room

Jeanne yawned. Once. Just once. As big a yawn as she could manage without dislocating her jaw. Her mother had always told her, "Be delicate when you yawn, Jeannie. A lady never shows her teeth or tongue." But then again, there was little about Jeanne that her mother ever approved of. And, in any case, there was no one in her bed now to see her yawn. There never was. So Jeanne yawned and smacked her lips in rebellion.

Jeanne scrunched her eyes up tighter and yawned once more, not because she needed to but to as a simple way to drive memories of her mother's incessant complaints out of her dreams. Nothing had been good enough for her mother. Not her daughter's yawns, nor her daughter's eating habits, her daughter's choice of employment, nor her daughter's big boobs and rounded shape, nothing had escaped Jeanne's mother. Everything that Jeanne was or did was wrong.

Jeanne pried her eyes open with a whispered, "Damn it all! I'm not going to sleep any longer, anyway." She gasped, and blinked rapidly. She shook her head once and then frantically glanced from one direction to another. She sucked air into her lungs driving her round breasts into the thick black strap that pushed their pillowy softness down her chest to overflow beneath the lower edge of the strap. Jeanne tried to move her hands but they too were bound to the metal cage beneath her. She screamed and twisted, trying desperately to tear herself free of the cage and the black straps that bound her to it. Back and forth, she twisted until she had no strength to continue. She lay there, eyelids peeled back from pupils that bounced from sight to sight, her hair spread in a tangle beneath her. Her chest heaved and her hands clenched and unclenched in time to the beat of her pounding heart.

"Where the fuck am I?" she screamed.

Jeanne slowly calmed enough to survey her surroundings. She lay on a metal frame with wire netting between the four solid strips. Well, not so much lay there as rested, somewhere between standing and a forty-five degree angle held upright by the heavy black straps. In front of her, she could see a corner where two grey metal walls met a grey ceiling. She could sense equipment behind her. Big, and heavy, it hummed in a low and steady drone. If Jeanne turned her head, she could just see others tied to platforms similar to the one that held her.

Story 1 The Engine Room

To her immediate right was a male, trussed as she was. His head lolled to the side, his black hair falling to cover his face. His chest was interesting, not overbuilt like a body builder but strong and well defined. Jeanne hummed as her eyes slowly traversed his chest. His stomach was rippled, and curved inward with just enough curve and softness to balance the hardness of his chest. Jeanne giggled as her eyes dropped lower. Strong thighs framed a shock of black hair and a longish prick. Soft now, it hung deliciously over his heavy balls. Jeanne hummed hungrily. She could feel her nipples harden and the area between her legs grow slick. Suddenly self-conscious, she licked her lips, and dragged her eyes away to explore the other inhabitants.

None were human. Beside the man, were four creatures Jeanne could have sworn were not even from Earth. The farthest two creatures were simple grey blobs. They rippled and undulated in a clear container. The two creatures between the man and the blobs looked alike. They had two legs (or so Jeanne thought of them) but six arms. Blue scales covered what appeared to be red skin. Four eyes dotted their upper torso, on either side of a fearsome set of teeth. One of the creatures had a long appendage that dangled from the rough center of its body. It flapped lazily against the creature's legs. The end of the appendage appeared almost to be a flower, long strips of multicolored skin encircling a bright red hole. The other creature had a short stub that protruded from between its legs.

Jeanne jumped as she heard a click from behind and to her left. Swinging her head quickly left her vision jumping and a ringing in her ears. She blinked rapidly and then slowly focused on the two creatures stepping through the open portal. They resembled nothing more than a pair of six foot tall Praying Mantis. Whip-like antennae topped a small triangular head. Large eyes formed each of the upper angles and tiny pincers formed the lower angle of the triangle. The tiny head topped a long thin body with four feet and two arms. Around the throat of each of them was a brass and steel medallion. This was their only concession to clothing, although the casing of each was in a slightly different shade of green.

"Come on, let's get a move on. We have to get this batch over to testing. I've just about had it with today. Almost got swarmed on that last planet, I did. Great Egg, what an infestation they have. Remind me to report it for culling. Anyway let's get on with this; I'm ready for a millipede stew and a fresh stack of grass."

Story 1 The Engine Room

"Could be worse. Some of these here beasties could'a' developed intelligence since we were last in this neck o' twigs."

"Don't even think it. Imagine an intelligent creature getting done to it what we're gonna do to these poor sods. Though I'd still be tempted to ignore the Translator, if you know what I mean. I don't want to stay here any longer than I have to and these here sods is our ticket out of this shithole."

"Ain't that the truth."

Jeanne stared at the bug-like creatures and then began screaming at them. Every swear word she could think of, every question she had, every demand to be released escaped in a solid tirade at the top of her voice. Still, the creatures continued to load the blob creatures, tipping them back, and then following behind their carts, occasionally steering by touching the cart with their tiny forelegs.

"Tired of yelling? It won't help you know. I've tried talking to them in English, German, and French. I even tried Welsh, and Gaelic. Nothing. Not a single blasted thing. Could just as well have been talking to a brick, for all the good it did. Hello, I'm Richard. Pleased to meet you. Even under these circumstances. Do forgive the inappropriate dress."

Jeanne looked at Richard, her eyes wide and her jaw open. She sputtered for a moment, and then gasped. Her face turned red and the blush slid down her neck and chest until her protruding breasts turned pink. She blinked and tried to stare at his face. His gorgeous deep brown eyes swallowed her, drawing her deep into their mirrored depths. When the fantasy of kissing his soft lips flickered through her brain, Jeanne shook her head and looked down. Unfortunately, what drew her eyes as she looked down was his long, hard cock. It now stood rigidly, poking out from between his thighs. The soft mushroom head was dark purple and swollen. A darker band encircled the thick rod just below the head. The main shaft was covered in thick veins that ballooned over the hardness. Jeanne blinked and licked her suddenly dry lips. The desire to kiss and lick that shaft was overwhelming.

"Umm, uh ... I'm Jeanne and fuck you're gorgeous. I mean, I'm sorry, I ... uh, oh fuck"

Story 1 The Engine Room

Richard laughed, deep and heavy, "Hello, Jeanne. Don't worry. Rather obviously, I feel the same way about you. Too bad, we didn't meet under better circumstances. You're a very beautiful woman and I'd love to spend time getting to know you. However, part of what you're feeling comes from a tube. They injected us while you were asleep. I noticed its effects almost immediately. Although with a bird as pretty as you, it might just have been nature working on its own. However, I don't believe so given our situation."

"What's happened? Where are we? What are they going ... "

Jeanne groaned as the Praying Mantis creatures entered the room once again. They walked behind two blue-scaled creatures and fiddled with a large box on the back of their beds for a moment. Then they slowly pushed the creatures, bed, and all around Jeanne and Richard, out the door and down the hall.

"Okay, you two. Off to the lab and the doc. Then it's off to the engines for you two. And we get to come back to pick up your roommates. Pick you up and push you over to the lab. Then back again, and rinse and repeat until shift ends. That's all we do all day.

Could'a' used a robot but no, has to be an intelligent being. Just in case one of you animals has growed some brains of your own. Not that I've got any brains in me head after doing this job all fuckin' day long. Rusted them out long ago. It's a wonder I can find my patch at night, it is. All's so we can go visit some shithole of a colony in the middle of fuckin' nowhere."

Jeanne listened as the two Praying Mantids bellyached their way down the corridor until their words disappeared in the echoes. Tears surged over her eyelids and dribbled down her cheeks to trickle along her lips in a salty trail. Her breath caught in hiccupping gulps. A shiver ran through her body, sending tremors rippling through her breasts where they swelled over the black straps. As her body trembled, a desire to curl into Richard's thick arms seized Jeanne. A need to feel his strong arms surrounding her, and his hot skin against hers filled her brain. The feel of his hot breath on her back slid down her spine. The need burned through her hips and ran along between her legs. She twisted in her bindings trying desperately to cross her legs but the straps on her ankles and thighs prevented her moving. The need grew and soon she was twisting and fighting the bonds. The need to have Richard holding her burned through her brain and down her neck, filling her chest with swelling foam blocks.

Story 1 The Engine Room

"Don't fight it, you'll just hurt yourself. I know. Just lay back and force yourself to calm. Count to 100. Focus on the corner of the room. Imagine choking your worst enemy. Anything, just don't look at me. Breathe slowly and deeply, and concentrate. You can control it. The need will calm down soon. Trust me. You just need to get past it. You can, you know. I have faith in you."

Richard's words jangled against her nerves. Pain shot through her eardrums and bounced between her eyeballs. Jeanne gasped as deeply as she could and grasped at the swell of calming air. Her teeth clenched and she tried desperately to push the air down through her air and out her screaming pussy, driving the unbearable need with it. She gulped at the air again and pushed, crying with the pain of fighting the unfathomable depths of her desire. Again and again, until the pain of her burning lungs slowly drained out her fingertips. With a final gasp, Jeanne collapsed in the straps. Her head hung on her chest, her hair in wet clumps plastered to her cheeks and forehead. Her eyes were closed, and tears streamed down her cheeks.

Jeanne gulped air as she slowly recovered from the need that still burned through her chest and stomach. Her clit itched and burned, and her pussy felt swollen and puffy. She could feel a stream of liquid dripping down her leg with every bleat of her thickened lips. Her legs shook with the intensity of her desire to shove something, anything between her legs. Jeanne whimpered as a burst of heat at the breast tips sent a wave of pain fleeing inwards along the nerves deep in her breasts to seize her heart in angry jaws, shaking and twisting it in her burning chest.

"Okay, a little better now? Be careful. You're still going to feel like a cat in heat for a while, but you should be able to control it."

Jeanne slowly raised her head. Her chest belled out with deep breaths that pushed the black strap deep into her breasts. The skin rolled out in angry red lines. Her angry brown nipples stood out well proud of the soft white skin. Jeanne's eyes slowly cracked opened. The sight of Richard's deep brown eyes filled with concern turned her pussy to mush. She could feel the soft tissues filling with liquid until they overflowed and her juices trickled down her leg. Jeanne dropped her eyes in embarrassment only to have them alight on the rock hard cock with the deep purple mushroom cap that pointed directly at her. Her tongue slipped out between dry lips as she imagined licking the hanging fruit swinging heavily from the black thicket between his legs. The tiny hole in the end of his hard purple limb

Story 1 The Engine Room

dragged on her eyes. The drop of liquid that gathered in the tiny indent called to her. Her mouth watered in response.

"Fuck me. Oh, God. Stick that hard cock deep in my pussy. Please. Fuck me. Now. Oh, God, fuck me so hard. Stick it in my cunt. Stick it in my ass. I wanna suck it. Oh, fuck me. I wanna cum. Please. Please."

Richard's cock jumped at Jeanne's words. The drop of pre-cum bellowed out and a long spider's string of liquid dripped to the floor. Richard whimpered. He gnawed at his lip, drawing blood that dribbled down his strong chin.

"It's the drug. You've got to fight it. If we give in to how much I want to stick my cock deep in your soft, wet pussy we'll never be able to escape. Oh God, I'll bet your pussy tastes so sweet. Fuck I want to stick my cock into your cunny."

A strong scent of ammonia, coriander, and mold rolled over Jeanne. A sudden burst of chittering clicks rattled the platform beneath her.

"Shit these two are noisy."

"Yeah, wonder what they're saying to each other?"

"Translator says it's just mating music. But damn, there's so fuckin' much of it. And it never seems to repeat. It's a wonder they ever manage to live long enough to mate if all they ever do is scream at each other. Oh well, ours not to wonder why. As long as they fit the profile. Let's get them hooked up. Lab says we don't need to test 'em. Their energy levels are high enough to screw the lab's reading even from here. Great Mother Egg, just imagine being that focused on reproducing. How the hell do they concentrate enough to even eat let alone hunt their own food?"

The banging and whirr of the machine behind Jeanne buried the sound of the alien's reply. A strong whiff of ammonia, coriander, and mold set Jeanne to sneezing as she felt a shuddering jolt. The platform squeaked as it rolled backwards into the corridor and then down the shadowed tube. Jeanne could hear an answering squeak from behind her as both metal frames with their soft human freight rolled down the shadowy tunnel.

Story 1 The Engine Room

The short trip ended in a room filled with tubes and wires. Black tubes and wires formed a solid mass around a clear space in the middle of the room. Two pairs of large hooks hung from the ceiling forming a corridor about two feet apart by six feet long. Metal shackles hung from thin poles the rose from the floor.

Jeanne's breath tore from her mouth as her platform twirled quickly about until she faced Richard. Her head continued to whirl long after her body stopped, leaving her stomach heaving in sympathy. She whimpered and her body shook in reaction. Her eyes closed as she fought the nausea. As the waves slowed, she cracked her eyelids to find herself focused on Richard's face. One look at Richard's concern and her stomach flipped again. This time it was lower and more pleasant. Her groin took up the clamping. Sensations bounced between the wet membranes and her stomach until the little bud began to scream in desire. Jeanne whimpered in need. She felt so empty and he had something to fill her up. It wasn't fair that he was so close and yet not inside her, filling her, fulfilling the need growing between her legs.

Jeanne screamed as she was ripped from Richard. The metal hooks banged off her platform and bounced before her. The wire cage beneath her cut into her skin as the platform halted suddenly. Sharp fingernails scraped across her back, weaving trails of cold and burning diamonds. The metal hooks banged on her breasts, cold fire across her soft flesh. Jeanne could barely focus her eyes as Richard was wheeled to rest in front of her.

The two Mantis-creatures slipped beside Richard and began to fiddle with the wires around him. The hooks were first. They were twisted and slipped behind him until the metal tips emerged beneath his armpits. Thick metal shackles attached to the poles snapped around his ankles. A belt slid beneath his back and then the mantis-thing buckled it around his stomach. The remaining metal cuffs clamped around his wrists with a metallic ping. A thick silver clasp locked his wrist between the belt and the silver metal wire running to the tall thin pole. The whole operation took less than a minute before the belts and shackles holding Richard to the platform were removed. One of the Praying Mantids pulled the platform out of the door. A humming noise accompanied the metal shackles pulling until Richard hung, legs apart, from the hooks.

The remaining Mantis thing skittered to Jeanne in a well-practiced move. While its partner stowed the platform, it hooked the shackles to her ankles and

Story 1 The Engine Room

wrists. Soon she too hung, legs apart, from the hooks. Jeanne blushed as she gazed at Richard, the pink glowing from her forehead down to her firm breasts topped with their hard brown buds. Confused her eyes flicked between his hard, bleating cock, his deep brown eyes, and his lips with their flickering tongue. Jeanne giggled as she noticed that try as he might to focus on her eyes, his own eyes kept sliding from her firm tits to her furry bush. His eyes lingered on the wet folds where they pulled apart by the spread of her legs. He panted and his tongue flicked over his lips. A soft whimper escaped from deep in his chest. His cock was hard and swollen, a long thin drip of pre-cum hanging from the purple tip.

Jeanne's eyes were dragged from admiring Richard by the prick of a needle in her arm. One of the Mantids had attached a long, thin, black tube to her arm. Another tube was soon inserted into her other arm, and a third was attached to the soft pad just above her round ass. Within moments, Jeanne could feel the desire build between her legs. It curdled and whirled across her mound and rattled against her spine. When the creature attached two thick tubes to her nipples, she screamed. She moaned as she felt the creature attach a thinner tube to the soft skin between her hip and her mound.

Jeanne hung quivering in her hooks. A long trail of spittle drooled down her lip and over her chin to drip on her soft breast. Her eyes flickered up to stare at Richard. His nurse was attaching the last of his tubes. Tubes grew from his arms, spine, and hip. Two thick tubes trailed from his nipples just as they did from her own. But the creature had also inserted a thick tube into his ass, past the tightly crinkled orifice she knew hid between his cheeks. While she watched, the creature seized his cock, that hard rod of flesh she wanted so badly and slipped a thick tube over the shaft. Two more tubes slid over his balls, one tube for each. Richard's head whipped back and forth, his eyes screwed tightly shut. His moans were higher and more frantic now. The creature seized his head, and forced the thickest tube yet over his mouth. Succeeding in its goal, it stepped back for a moment and basked in its artistry.

Jeanne screamed as she felt a thick something push against her rectum. It filled the space between her ass-cheeks and slowly rotated around the crinkled sensitive flesh. Hot liquid spurted into her, past the tightly clenched sphincter, leaving her inner body oily and slick. Whatever the tube was, it caught on her flesh and squirmed past the tight guardian. Thin at first it sent waves of vibration tumbling through her lower body. Jeanne moaned and whimpered as the sensations

Story 1 The Engine Room

overwhelmed a body already close to overload. Slowly the thing swelled, vibrating and throbbing within her. Soon her body felt as if she was filled from the back, the excess flesh pushed into her thrumming cunt.

The double tube the creature pushed into Jeanne's pussy was almost an anti-climax. It slid past her lips, and over the liquid-covered ridges, stretching her cunny and filling her emptiness. The tinier of the two tubes slipped upwards to wiggle beneath the hood that protected her center. When they, too, began to pulse and vibrate, Jeanne gulped and gasped. Her eyes slowly focused on Richard's groin. He flexed his hips and vibrated to the pleasures he must have been feeling. The tube attached to his penis pulsed and swallowed as he whimpered. Jeanne moaned in sympathy as she felt a tube attack her mouth. Its probe tickled across her lips, probing her teeth and then retreating.

"Eggshells, you're slow. Let's get the brain distenders attached and then we can call it a day. On three. One. Two. Three."

Jeanne felt a thick band surround her forehead, and then her brain filled with whirling colors. She could still see Richard, as he hung from the hooks, his cock and balls, mouth, and nipples hooked to thick, black, pulsating tubes. Slowly a picture of Richard approaching, his hard cock naked and pointed at her overlaid the reality. Richard's bouncing cock mesmerized her until she started when she realized he stood before her. His wet lips slid down to hers. His brown eyes slowly closed as his tongue fought with hers for entrance to her mouth.

Jeanne could feel the others waiting impatiently behind her. But her every thought was with Richard now. He was her man. He would be the first to enter her, his hard shaft sliding deep into her body, filling her. But for now, all she knew was he was kissing her. Deep and strong, his tongue pushed past her teeth. It battered at her defenses and then slid along her palate. It tickled at her uvula and trailed over her tongue. Jeanne's breath caught and she sucked hard at the invader, pulling at the wet skin. She panted her need, tasting his in their oral battle. Whimpers slid around swollen flesh.

Jeanne gasped, her mouth wide, as she collapsed under Richard's assault. Need flowed up her throat and over her lips, to flow in a hot breath down his chest. He slid her mouth down, down his hard chest,

Story 1 The Engine Room

past his sharply pointed nipples, past the indent of his navel in his rounded tummy, past the bush of black hair. Jeanne cried as she sought to suckle only to be rushed past all those very tasty spots until her mouth slid against his rigid pole. She could feel the soft sacks hanging below. They banged slowly against her chin in a demand to be let in. She could taste the mix of salt and sweet flesh at the base of his prick. Her clit screamed, demanding she fill her mouth with the hot, hard rod. Almost as if she was punishing her body for her need, Jeanne licked along the hot shaft, teasing herself with the tastes. Her lips slid a hair's breadth above the soft flesh, her tongue flicking out to tickle the sensitive skin.

Jeanne could feel Richard's need now. It flowed through his softly bouncing cock, through her flicking tongue and filled her mouth and head. It danced with her own desire, flaring in bursts of lightning behind her eyes and flashes of burning heat between her thighs. Jeanne's tongue slipped over his softness, twirling against the ballooning veins that lined his hard shaft. She licked along his corona, teasing between the shaft and soft bulb of his glans. With a moan, she slipped her mouth over the mushroom head and pushed until his entire shaft was buried within her mouth. Her lips mumbled against his pubic mound, scraping the stray hairs against the sensitive flesh. With a gasp, she bucked back leaving the hard shaft of flesh bouncing in its desire to be buried once again.

Jeanne nibbled on the soft purple head. Her tongue flicked against the hole in the end of his glans, sliding along the groove, and tasting his salty desire. She bit and chewed for a moment, reveling in the taste and feeling of control, then chewed her way down the shaft, licking and sucking as his cock bounced between tongue and palate. Jeanne hummed, driving the vibration along the hard rod. Rolling her lips over her teeth, she pulled back along his shaft until just the tip remained in her hot, sucking mouth. With a moan, she dived again driving the soft fleshly half sphere against her palate, scraping it along her tongue. Jeanne sucked on the shaft that seemed to drive deep into her throat. Her cheeks worked as she drew out the salty musky sweet juices. Up and down, she slid on his shaft, sucking steadily until his body began to jerk in a slow rhythm. His balls bounced against her chin and his hairs tickled her nose until she felt like she was going to sneeze. His shaft flexed and bounced within her mouth.

Jeanne seized the hot, wet shaft. Her hand stripped up and down, the wetness from her saliva flowing out through her clenched fingers. Her tightly clenched hand slammed against his groin and then fled

Story 1 The Engine Room

to bounce against her lips where they were locked around his corona. Each impact on her lips sent an explosion of sensation through the soft glans trapped within her mouth and down the aching shaft. Jeanne giggled and pulled her mouth off the hard shaft. Her eyes glistened as she ran the soft, wet bulbous head down her chin, over her neck and then down her soft body. She played for a time with his cock against her soft breast, teasing her hard nipples against the softness. She fought for a moment, to force the hard bud into the hole in the end of his cock, but with a mew of impatience, dragged the hard rod down her body. She dragged the long shaft through her bush, knowing that the hard hairs would feel like knife blades on his sensitive skin. Then she forced the hard shaft lower to caress her hot, wet folds. The soft tip dragged on the loose flesh of her inner lips as she dragged the rod along her cleft. She screamed as the heat flamed across her clit. She winced as his bouncing hips drove her prize against her soft flesh.

"Shit, handsome. Be careful. That's as high as it goes. You've run out of room. Give me a second and you'll be able to push as much as you like."

Richard panted in reply. His panting had turned to whimpers and he trembled in her hands. Jeanne grinned, her eyes shining as she felt her prey sliding into her trap. The soft head dragged at her wet folds as she forced his hard shaft to that spot above her cavern. She pushed on his shaft, forcing the soft mushroom bulb to squeeze past her flesh. Forced the softness to slide over her wet folds. Forced her glistening skin to swell over the shaft. She pushed until the hard shaft slipped deep into her pussy. Richard's hips pounded her body as his body realized the way was now clear. Her hand was trapped, forced against her mound, intensifying the sensations until she dragged the crushed limb out from between their sweaty bodies. Jeanne shivered, bouncing as the sensations from the hard thickness rattled through her groin and up her back.

Richard bounced against her mound. His hard cock drove deep into Jeanne, crashing against her insides with a mix of pain and joy. His thickness dragged at her clenching folds, stretching her, sliding on her flesh, sending flashes of heat lightning exploding through her lower body. Jeanne screamed at the invader, urging it on, urging it deeper, urging it to swell deep within her, forcing the crisis to explode deep within her body.

Story 1 The Engine Room

Jeanne moaned as she felt the other slide in behind her. His hands caressed her back, sliding over her spine and along her shoulders. His hands slid down her arms and then seized her ass. The heat from his hands burned through her skin. It fried her gluteus maximus with burning need, driving deep shafts of desire through the firm flesh. Jeanne could feel her skin stretch painfully as he forced the cheeks apart, revealing her hidden hole. She could feel Richard smashing into her mound, ripples of the impacts spreading up her ass. Surely, he didn't intend ... ? This stranger standing behind her couldn't possibly ...

Jeanne screamed as she felt the invader pry her crinkled hole apart. She could feel the mushroom end of his cock crushing against her asshole, pushing the sphincter apart as the hard shaft crushed the soft helmet into her body. A mix of pleasure and pain screamed through her lower body as hardness met hardness with her need crushed between. Desire squeezed from need in explosions of color and fire and sound that burst from her clit and flamed up her spine to explode from her throat.

Caught between the two crushing rods, Jeanne screamed her need, her words turning into bubbles of sound that exploded from a mouth gone slack with desire. She stared at the ceiling, losing her sanity in the sensations that burned upwards from her straining cunt and ass. And still the two hard cocks pounded her soft flesh, driving the need to overflow, leaving her legs shaking in the confusion of her overwhelmed nerve endings. Richard's hard cock slid over her moist tissues, dragging on the soft flesh, stretching her. Every impact of his hardness on her soft inner core sent a flash of sensation burning through her brain.

Behind her, the stranger drove his cock deep into Jeanne's bowels. Sometimes in synchronicity with Richard, more often out of step. He pounded deep into her sensitive flesh, sending ripples of sensation flooding over her hips and body. Every impact drove his cock against Richard's hardness with only Jeanne's thin membranes crushed between. Every stroke sent sensations crushing through Jeanne that left her eyes crossed and her mouth open. Jeanne's head hung, her tongue lolling out of her mouth, spittle dribbling down her tongue and dripping on the hard cock that pounded at her cunt.

Three heads flung back with a crack. Three mouths screamed at the heavens. Three bodies convulsed under the assault of sensations of release and joy and pleasure. Three bodies bounced under

Story 1 The Engine Room

waves of fire and heat exploding from three groins. Jeanne could feel the hot liquid shooting deep into her body. She could feel her body convulse with joy at the hot fire bouncing off tissues made supersensitive with the fire of her emotions. She screamed again and again, until with a moan she collapsed and hung slowly convulsing as lessening waves of pleasure rolled over her. She shivered as she felt Richard's cock pull out with a soft pop. She whimpered as she felt his tongue slide down her body, licking for a moment at her aching nipples before continuing downwards.

* * *

Richard and Jeanne hung from the hooks in the middle of a room filled with black tubes. Their bodies slowly convulsed, shaking in their reactions. Sweat rolled down their backs. Fluids bubbled around the tubes and dribbled down their legs. Around them, the black tubes glowed and pulsed with a purple light.

* * *

The cockpit windows showed the bright rounded edge of a blue planet outlined in the blackness of deep space. Three of the Praying Mantis creatures stood around the flight deck, flicking switches and studying video readouts.

"Batteries are already at 100%. Charging rate is right off the scale. It's those damn humans. Their sexual energy is too much for our systems. I don't know if we can handle these rates in flight, Captain. But I do know that we need to leave now or start discharging excess, Sir."

"Aye, aye, Engineer. We don't have much of a choice if we're going to get to the colony. Pilot, engage engines. Get us out of here."

"Aye, aye, Captain. Engaging mass-local engines. Warp engines are going to full charge and ready. Prepare for gravity bump in five, four, three, two ... Mass-local engaged. Warp in ten centrons."

"Engage as soon as we leave the gravity well. Let's go see our colony mates, mantids. And pray we can burn energy as fast as those creatures can create it. And that they can last as long as the stories claim."

2. Steamy Knickers

Preface

Way back in Steamy Shorts 1 I introduced the characters of Messrs. Hardshaft, Taws & Cie. in a story called, funnily enough, Steamy Shorts. It was one of my earliest stories written for the collection (although under a different name), and I fell in love with the characters. I also fell in love with their names. Victorian porn can be quite silly with their character names and I, quite frankly, had a little too much fun with this crew of horny employees.

I knew as soon as I finished the first story that there was more there. That I would have the characters bugging me, waking me up, and otherwise nagging me until I told the rest of their stories. It's the way characters work. Ask any writer. But that's only part of the story of the story.

Every once in a while, I will get a scene or situation stuck in my head. I can't get rid of it until I write it. I did say that I was a little strange, didn't I? That scene/situation/position/view combined with my friends from Messrs. Hardshaft, Taws & Cie.. Every time I turned around Lilly and Mr. Taws were finding some reason to end up in a particular position performing that particular movement. Even actually putting Toy in that position didn't get them to stop. (I know TMI). They kept finding story after story to end up with that particular position. Usually while I was trying to sleep.

This is one of the stories. Between the characters and the scene it demanded to be written. So I've done it. I've written it, and I've even published it. Now, Messrs. Hardshaft, Taws, and Lord Whyp, Misses Lucy, Josey, and of course our dear sweet Lilly, would you please shut up and let me sleep?

Steamy Knickers

Lilly swung down from the omnibus to land on the cobblestone sidewalk in a cloud of steam that billowed out around her. Her one hand clutched at the ornate brass handhold as she wobbled on the uneven brickwork. Her other hand clutched a silk bobbin lace handkerchief scrunched against the leather goggles that hid her green eyes from view. The white silk lace trailed over her mouth and nose and down her chin. Wisps of white steam slipped through her bright red hair to form a halo around the tiny black flowerpot hat that perched on one side of her head.

The steamer-bus growled off in a black-streaked, white cloud and a high-pitched jangle of bells. Lilly weaved unsteadily on the uneven pavers. Her black thigh-high boots and her tight jade-green velvet skirt conspired to remove any balance she might possess on the red bricks. Crowds of middle and lower class workmen surged and eddied around her, their focus on their jobs not the upper class lady who blocked the pathway. With a burst of energy, Lilly shook her shoulders and straightened her spine. She tumbled forward and half-ran, half-fell toward the black marble building a half-block before her.

A strong, muscular arm caught her around the waist and dragged her clutching and grasping form up as a particularly nasty cobblestone jumped up and tripped her. Lilly found her breasts pressed against the thick, red serge wool coat of the doorman. Her jaw was propped on his shoulder and she stared at the oversized brass doors of Messrs. Hardshaft, Taws & Cie. with its gold picked metal plate. The three devil headed gargoyles stared disapprovingly down at her antics.

"Careful there, Miss Whyte. You don't want to fall and scrape those pretty knees of yours. Are you all right?"

"Yes, thank you, Edward. I'm afraid these boots aren't particularly well designed for alighting from steamers onto cobbles. I should be thankful I didn't twist my ankle."

"Yes, Ma'am. I'm sure Mr. Taws would be quite upset if you had injured yourself. I don't know why you don't just let him supply you with a horse and driver or a steamer of your own, Ma'am. It would be safer and more pleasant."

Story 2 Steamy Knickers

"True, but less independent. And how can I expect him to respect my independence if I don't take the bad with the good?"

"As you say, Miss. As you say."

Lilly levered herself off the thick muscular chest of the doorman. She adjusted her black velvet shrug and then carefully climbed the steps to stand before the heavy brass doors. She smiled and nodded her head in acknowledgement to the doorman's efforts and then slid between the oppressive weights of brass. The click of her boot heals on the white marble floors echoed off the walls of black marble, streaked with gold. The dull thud of the heavy door swelled over her and echoed around the elegant foyer.

Lilly smiled as she approached the iron cage of the elevator at the far side of the foyer. A young woman in her early twenties stood erect before the ornate, gilded-iron gate. She smiled shyly and curtseyed as Lilly approached. Her breasts trembled beneath the semi-transparent silk of her simple blouse. Her hard nipples puckered the silk, pink circles hinted at beneath the white gossamer. Gold circles showed plainly beneath the silk. A gold cameo of three men's heads swung from a black choker locked tightly around her neck.

Lilly smiled wider as she passed the young woman. One hand reached up to toy with the gold cameo of a single man's head on her own choker. Her other hand reached out to seize the woman's breast and her thumb flicked over the hard button. The woman whimpered and her legs quivered. Her hips flexed from side to side and her long, black bustle skirt slid from side to side. The rolled front emphasized the rolling of her hips as it crushed and spread to her movements.

"I presume your tether is in, Elsie? And functioning well?"

"Yes, Miss Whyte. Miss Hittenlick and Miss Bunnybut 'ave been up and down several times on errands already this mornin'. Miss Hittenlick turned the machinery to full speed when she arrived, if'n it meets your approval, Miss. I'm not sure I could take it if it was working any better, Miss."

"Show me. And I'll observe as you operate the lift."

Story 2 Steamy Knickers

"Yes, Miss," Elsie squeaked.

Both women entered the metal cage of the lift. Lilly continued to squeeze Elsie's breast, her finger flicking over Elsie's hard nipple. Elsie bleated at every flick as she fiddled with the control stick. A whimper burst from Elsie's lips as the steam engines below roared to life. As the lift shook and rattled, Elsie reached before her and rolled the skirt up until soft flesh and a thick red bush peeped beneath the material.

A long thick tube ran from the lift's control, up her leg and then disappeared into the warm flesh between her legs. A thinner tube snaked from her leg up and around and into the pink, bare lips where they came together below the red bush. Elsie's flesh shook and rumbled as a whirring noise came from her lower body. Occasional puffs of steam spurted from the contraption. Elsie whimpered and gasped as her body shook. Her head banged against the cage and she grasped the gold sconces set above her head. Lilly continued to rub her nipple, flicking over the hard flesh, and pulling on the gold hoop.

Lilly slid her hand over the soft silk, seeking the ruffled ridge that guarded the soft heat beneath.

Her fingers fought with the roundness of the pearls for a moment of frustration and then slid the soft, slick material back around the pointed hills of Elsie's breasts. Her hand squeezed a soft mound, forcing the pointed nipple to protrude out, seeking the hot contact of mouth and teeth. Lilly's tongue flicked out, circling the soft, hardness. It tripped over the bumps and pulled on the cold gold circlet. She sucked hard on the flesh, drawing a moan deep from Elsie's chest.

Lilly slid her other hand down, down over the soft warmth of Elsie's belly, over the roughness of the bunched skirt, and through the scratchiness of her bush. Lilly groaned as she felt the catches of the stubble along Elsie's shaved skin. Softness and warmth warred with the sharpness until her fingers slid into the wet heat. Lilly's fingers played in the folds and over the hard lump with its tube sliding into the hooded flesh, bouncing over the sensitive lump. The tube vibrated against Lilly's fingers, sending vibrations down into Lilly's fingertips where they shook deep within Elsie. Lilly's hand oscillated over the soft flesh, driving her palm against Elsie's mound with every movement. Lilly's mouth drew on her hard aching nipple in time, dragging the flesh as if it could meet in the center where sensations met and exploded in bursts of light and electricity.

Story 2 Steamy Knickers

Elsie screamed as the cage ground to a halt, the lift stopping with the heavy thunk of gears being thrown over. Her body went rigid and she ground her back against the cold iron cage. Her hands turned white against the gold sconces, as she fought to hold herself upright. Her toes were pointed, and she shook against the iron, setting the metal to jangling. With a groan, all strength fled from her body and she collapsed to lay senseless in a jumble of cloth and skin.

Lilly straightened. She pulled on the arms of her shrug, straightening the deep green velvet jacket. Her hands slid over the jade-green skirt, removing any disturbance to how it hugged her form. The crisp white blouse was next, sliding the soft silk over her distended nipples. Finally, the waist of the shrug received one last tug. Lilly gazed down on the blubbering form and smiled. With a huff of pleasure, she reached out and slid the gilded-iron gate open.

As she strode through the gate, her boots made a clicking noise on the marble floors that continued the clicking of the gate sliding open. An answering series of clicks caused her to look up as a pretty, tall, blonde woman slid to a stop in front of her. The woman's hands flew over her clothing, straightening waistbands, and patting errant wisps of hair. An undone button led to a flurry of hands, pushing and prodding at the white, silk blouse. Her nipples danced proudly visible through the silk. The gold cameo of a man at her throat bounced in laughter. Her face was flushed and blotched. Patches of red dappled across her cheeks, and forehead. She panted and her legs shook as she slid to a stop. Her fingertips dabbed at her lips.

"Oh, it's just you. Good morning, Lilly. I'm glad you're here. Josey is off on an errand, and My Lord is upset with how I folded his morning newspaper. You've caught us in the middle of my punishment, I'm afraid. Could you watch the lift, please? Just until Josie returns. It's her turn, you see. I'm afraid I'm not going to be good for much this morning. His Lordship is in fine form, and I'm unlikely to be able to sit comfortably for quite some time. Thank you. You're an absolute dear. Sorry to rush, but punishment and pleasure await. And I wouldn't want dear Whyppie to get bored and wander off. Ta, ta."

With a rub of both hands on her round posterior, the young woman turned and ran off the way she had come. Lilly giggled. After a year of working for Mr. Taws, Lilly still marveled at Lucy Hittenlick's energy. How the studious and quiet Lord Whyp could contain the minx was quite beyond her. She was obviously very

Story 2 Steamy Knickers

good or she wouldn't have been working for such a prestigious firm. But still, she always seemed to be on the verge of complete and total disarray in the face of a terrible exigency. Lilly shook her head in disbelief.

Lilly turned and started to walk down the corridor to her office. Before she reached the limits of the reception office she stopped and turned to look back at Elsie piled in the corner of the lift. Lilly rubbed her chin and murmured quietly. With a jerk of her head, she moved back to the lift. She reached through the gate, and pushed the lever on the lift downwards. Quickly bouncing back, she pulled the cage gate closed in a stream of clacks and clicks. A second set of clicks and clacks marked the closing of the floor's safety gate. As the lift growled and rumbled to life, a loud moan wafted up from the mound of clothing and skin on the lift's floor.

Lilly turned and walked off into the offices, secure in the knowledge that the lift would stop automatically at street level. There were only two levels for that lift, after all. So it was child's play to rig the control to stop at the thirtieth floor and street level. There really wasn't a reason to have a human operator at all, Lilly knew. But the occasional visitor expected to see a lift operator and besides, Elsie was such a brilliant distraction when the bosses were away.

Lilly looked slowly around her office. She knew every inch of the luxurious space, from its thick Turkish rug to the dark walnut desk. She knew it from the deep maroon walls to the dark walnut wainscoting. It too had changed over the last year as her employer, Mr. Taws, had redecorated her office to be more and more a miniature version of his own. Lilly moued at the result. It was a little touch masculine for her taste. Still, it succeeded at being expensive without being ostentatious. A few feminine touches were still needed, but Lilly was determined to soften the lines without going over the top as so many of her friends would have. Moreover, she was in no great hurry. After all, this was a business office not her boudoir or her drawing room. Visions of lace and decorations flitted through her thoughts and were quickly rejected, as she stripped her velvet shrug off shoulders and hung the tiny coat carefully behind the main door.

Lilly leaned against the sideboard and poked her head through the inner door. Neither exactly within the spirit, nor, on the other hand, was she precisely violating her employer's rule about entering his office. Lilly was certain that he refrained from being annoyed

Story 2 Steamy Knickers

only because he enjoyed her interesting solution to bending his rules. The swell of her breasts as they swung to the side beneath her blouse was also a help, she was certain.

Since Mr. Taws had yet to appear, Lilly began her usual morning ritual. Check any work left over from the previous day. Check both her and her employer's diaries to determine if there were any scheduled tasks today. File any unfiled work from the previous day. Run a duster over the furniture and books. And finally, make tea.

The water had just been put to boil, when the bell announcing the lift rang. Lilly strolled to the reception. She took up her usual waiting position, her back rigid, and her head held high. Her perfectly controlled form faced the lift with her hands cupped before her. The large, formal picture of Queen Victoria stared disapprovingly over her shoulder. With difficulty, Lilly controlled her desire to tap her foot in irritation at the delay. She didn't have long to wait before the metal cage dinged to a stop with a rattle.

Within the lift, stood Josephine Bunnybut. Josey, to her friends, had her legs apart as far as her tight skirt allowed, and her back was braced against the iron cage. Her red hair was, as usual, perfectly coiffured with nary a hair out of place. A swelling at the front of her red skirts pulsated with a regular rhythm. Josey moaned softly, her breasts swelling and falling erratically. The engines for the lift continued their growling while a soft whimpering came from beneath the swelling. Lilly coughed softly and Josey turned her head. Her eyes slowly focused on her silent observer.

"Oh, hello Lilly. I noticed poor Elsie in a state and decided to take advantage. Unfortunately, Mr. Hardshaft is visiting clients today and I'm quite beside myself with inactivity. I gather dear Lucy has been naughty since you are acting as greeter. Thank you. I should finish in a very few moments. I'm quite close. I'll take over the duties shooorrrtlllyyy."

Lilly shook her head and smiled at Josey's scream as she turned to wander back to her own duties. After all, Mr. Taws would soon be appearing. And today was the day that Lilly would discover who had won the wager. Lilly grinned as she thought back over the past month. How Mr. Taws had bent her over his desk for a minor infraction. How his hand on her globes had felt. How she had spread and pushed to meet him. How the discussion afterward had

Story 2 Steamy Knickers

progressed to a disagreement over the best investment for an important client. How the disagreement had culminated in a wager. Whose investment would produce the best return in the next month?

Lilly smiled and blushed. At times John Taws could be so blind, but at other times, he could see right to her heart with a clarity that quite astounded her. She had often wondered what it would have been like if their positions were reversed. If she had the crop and he were bent over the desk. He had chosen to indulge her curiosity for his part of the wager. On the other hand, he had been cryptic about her payment to him if he had won. All he would say is that she must agree to his demand if he won. As if she could deny him anything. The year she had spent in his employ had been the most pleasurable of her short life. Absolute foolishness. For the past month, she prodded him to tell her his part of the wager. He, for his part, had adamantly refused to answer. Instead, he teased her until she grew careless and pushed him too far. Then he would have to punish her for her impertinence. Lilly smiled at the memories. Her hips shifted in response.

Lilly shook out the first of the day's newspapers, picked up her scissors and began to scan. Each time she found an article on one of the topics Mr.

Taws had an interest in, or an article on the firm itself, she cut it out, marked the date and source, and then placed it in a folder. Soon she had several folders filled with articles. Within a few hours, the pile of newspapers had shrunk considerably, and the file folders were piled high on the corner of her desk.

Lilly raised her arms and stretched, her firm breasts lifting and pushing against the thin silk of her blouse. Her eyes shut, she continued to twist, and groan until the thoughts of her tea growing cold penetrated her tired mind. As she reached for the forgotten teacup, she noticed John Taws leaning against the doorframe. A gentle smile stretched his black mustache beneath misty blue eyes and his strong patrician nose. Flecks of grey dotted his carefully combed black hair. His tight grey waistcoat hinted at the strong chest she knew lay beneath the crisp white cotton shirt and collar. Black trousers completed the ensemble, stretching his powerful thighs down to the shiny black shoes.

"Oh, sir. I'm sorry. I didn't notice you. I'm afraid I was focused on the clippings. Is there anything I can help you with, Mr. Taws? A cup of tea, perhaps? Or dictation?"

Story 2 Steamy Knickers

"No, Miss Whyte. I was just enjoying watching you concentrate. I often do that, you know. Watch you as you work. You do make focusing on my own work difficult, after all. And I believe we have a wager to decide this morning. So I'm afraid I'm a little more distracted than is usually the case."

Lilly's smiled widely, sparkles lighting up her eyes, and a dusting of red coloring her rounded cheeks. Her head cocked slightly and she looked down at the floor by his feet. With a soft harrumph, she turned and stood, her back straight. She walked to the sideboard, checked the dial on the side of the Richardson Automatic Tea Making Appliance, and pressed the button. The brass and cherry wood creation began to hiss and steam. By the time, she had placed a fresh cup beneath the spout, a stream of hot, strong tea was pouring out. Two lumps of sugar soon followed into the brown mixture. With the tiny clatter of fine china, Lilly carried the steaming result over to Taws.

"You really don't need to do that, you know. I'm quite capable of making my own cup of tea. I did spend ten years in rather more uncivilized parts of the empire, after all. Why, we even had to add our own milk and boil the water in a proper kettle."

Lilly stared up at her employer, her breasts almost touching his chest, and a disgusted look plastered on her face. His breath came faster and he shifted uncomfortably. Her own nasal passages flexed as she breathed in his scent of musk and old books.

"I'm well aware that you are quite capable. However, it is my pleasure to serve you. And I intend to do so. You, sir, will sit back, enjoy it, and accept it with appropriate expressions of pleasure as befits a proper gentleman. I shall be Mother. And you will not take that pleasure away from me."

"As you wish," Taws gulped.

"You have no appointments today, and the results of the market trades should be available shortly. Since you have brought up the matter of our wager, when you are ready to settle, I would be pleased to prove that mine were the better choices."

"Yes, well, as to that. I'm waiting for the delivery of a package. There was a slight delay, I'm afraid. As soon as it arrives, I shall be pleased to discuss the terms of settlement."

Story 2 Steamy Knickers

"In that case, unless you have something better for me to do, I shall return to my tea and my proper duties."

Lilly grinned up at her employer. She turned sharply, her shoulder and arm rubbing across his chest and stomach. She stomped back to the sideboard and the teasmade. A hissing and the clink of a single sugar cube signaled Lilly's return to her desk. The quiet laugh from Taws signaled his slow wander back to his desk.

It was approaching the noon hour when the lift bell rang once again. Some moments later, the sound of the lift arriving filtered through Lilly's consciousness and she looked up from the article on the recent invention of a clockwork servant. The device showed great promise and Lilly had suggested approaching the inventor, a Doctor P., with the offer of development capital. Moments later the click of Josey Bunnybut's heels on the marble floors approached Lilly's door.

"Mr. Taws's delivery has arrived. They are both superb. The boy insisted on showing them to me. He was quite proud of his master's efforts. Justifiably so. Mr. Taws will want to see them immediately. Tell Mr. Taws, I'm sure they'll do a treat."

Lilly looked up just as Josey placed a plain brown cardboard box on her desk. Lilly stared as Josey curtsied and then walked back to her desk, her head turned to watch Lilly's reaction. So focused was she on Lilly's reaction, Josey barely avoided walking into the doorjamb as she left. Left to go back to her cream, if the pussy's smile was any indication, thought Lilly. Most strange.

With a shake of her head, Lilly picked up the box and examined it. It was a plain brown box with no maker's mark, sealed with rather heavy twine and blue sealing wax, about ten inches in length, an inch and a half in width, and slightly shorter in height. When Lilly shook it, while she could feel something shift, there was no sound. With a tiny frown of curiosity, Lilly stood up and carried the package to Mr. Taws's door. She knocked on the doorframe, and then stood waiting for his response. Her head was erect, her back straight, and her breasts pushed into the doorway as if eager to enter her employer's domain. One hand held the package across her stomach, while the other was bent behind her. As her employer looked up, Lilly dipped her head.

"Ah, it's here. Excellent. I overheard Miss Bunnybut's evaluation. I'm eager to examine it myself.

Story 2 Steamy Knickers

Please place it on the desk. If you would obtain the results of our investments from Miss Bunnybut, I will be available to settle our wager in a moment."

Lilly placed the package on the desk in front of Mr. Taws, while he rooted amongst the knickknacks on his bookshelves for a knife. She curtsied and then backed out of the room, watching him with curiosity while he sliced open the parcel, and then waited pointedly for her to leave. Once clear of his office, she turned and strode purposefully towards Josey.

Lilly arrived at Josey's desk to find Josey, Lucy, and Elsie whispering and giggling. The three conspirators silenced as Lilly approached. Lilly scrutinized the three and frowned. Elsie had her fist in her mouth to ensure silence. Lucy blushed and her shoulders shook. Only Josey maintained her reserve as she handed Lilly a sealed envelope without being asked. As Lilly strode back to her office, she could hear the giggles and high pitched squeals begin once again.

Lilly stood before the door to Mr. Taws's office and took a deep breath. She shook her shoulders, loosening the knots that had formed just below her neck. She could feel her tits roll from side to side, the firm caps hardening against the soft silk. With a last puff of breath, she straightened her back and knocked on the doorjamb. She waited impatiently at the entrance to her employer's domain with her legs apart, and her head bent. One arm twisted behind her, grasping the waistband of her skirt. The other held the envelope before her. She fought to keep from tapping her foot but she could feel her body reacting to the discipline of waiting.

It seemed to Lilly as if an hour had passed, but it could only have been a few moments when she heard the voice she knew so well telling her to come in. Lilly strode in and placed the sealed envelope on the desk before her employer. She remained standing before the desk, her legs spread as far as her skirt allowed, both arms behind her back, and her head bent. She could hear the creak of his chair, but could not see Mr. Taws. She did notice that the package no longer sat on the desk. Her nose wrinkled in curiosity and her lips flexed from side to side. Still, she remained in place, unmoving, as she awaited her employer's pleasure.

The movement of Mr. Taws's hands at the edge of her sight almost brought a gasp from her. She could feel her heart speed and her breath catch in her throat. She could feel her chest heave at the sudden movement. The flick of a knife on the envelope made a hissing sound as it slid along the fold and then prised the seal and envelope apart with a soft crack.

"Bloody Hell! Bugger me, but you did it. Look at these figures. Don't just stand there, come around."

Lilly looked up to see Mr. Taws staring at her, his mouth open and an incredulous look on his face. Two pages of figures lay on the desk between his hands. One had the name of one of Mr. Taws's bigger clients at the top. The other had Mr. John Taws written in the customer's position. While both amounts were quite sizeable, the amount on his personal account's sheet was considerably higher. Lilly stared at the amount in disbelief.

"Oh, my word. I've actually won. I beat you."

"You did indeed, my girl. You did indeed."

"Wait a moment; this is a real account sheet. You mean, you invested on my suggestion? But ..."

"Of course, I believe in you. Always and forever. And between the commission from this and your salary, I expect your dowry will be quite sizeable as a result."

"Commission? I am not paid a commission. I meant that I have won our bet, sir. And you must pay the penalty."

"Oh, and what do you propose."

"Since you have underestimated my strengths I shall have to teach you that I am rather stronger than you expect. Trousers and underthings down and bent over the table. You know the position; you've had me in it quite frequently. Now, sir!"

Mr. Taws stood, a shocked look on his face. Though, in fact, his eyes danced and flashes of a smile tugged at his cheeks. He stared at Lilly for a long moment. With a snort, he stomped to the end of the table, which stood, in the middle of his office. With a flourish, he loosened his belt and suspenders, and dropped his trousers into a puddle at his feet. Lilly noted that the shorts, which peaked from beneath his shirttails, were quite colorful. Soon the reds and deep blues formed a second puddle at his feet.

"Down, sir, on your stomach. Your arms above you. Quickly now. No lollygagging about."

Lilly quickly secured Mr. Taws's arms above his head with straps that attached to the table for that purpose. She petted his head, and then caressed his back, trailing her hand along his body as she moved to stand behind him. She could feel his skin ripple beneath her fingertips. She bent down to remove the clothes from around his legs, but quickly thought the better of it. Standing and walking to the opposite end of the table, she raised Mr. Taws's head by the simple expedient of grabbing a quantity of his hair and pulling. Placing his chin on the table, she fiddled with her own waistband for a moment. The heavy material soon slid down her legs and puddled at her own feet.

Lilly stood before him. Her shapely legs were covered in black boots. The heels were five inches high and thick. The lower portions were laced with leather ribbon from the foot to just above the ankle. The soft leather hugged her calves and broke at her knees. Black leather reached above to roll over at her mid-thighs.

They formed the perfect frame to the soft pink peaking from under Lilly's own silken shirttails. Mr. Taws moaned.

Lilly kicked her feet free of her skirt. With a snicker, she strode to the opposite end of the table, and then knelt on her heels. She stared at his strong thighs for a long moment, resisting the urge to stare at the soft skin sack that hung between. With a puff of outblown air, she raised and lowered both arms quickly, striking down at the rounds covered in soft, white cotton. Mr. Taws grunted at the impact. Lilly held the round flesh for a moment, then, slowly lowered her hands, she traced the strong thighs. Her thumbs almost met in the middle, scraping the flesh lightly with her fingernails. Reaching his knees, her hands began the return journey. This time they travelled under the cotton shirttails. Her fingernails scraped the hot flesh of his thighs. Her thumb knuckles almost touched, pushing the soft flesh out of the way.

As Lilly's hands reached the top of the round globes, she seized the cotton material and scrunched it up to lie over Mr. Taws's back. Out of the way of both hands and eyes, it formed a ridge between Mr. Taws as a person and the parts that Lilly's mind and body were drawn to. Her hands slid up beneath the shirt, and Lilly smiled as she felt his skin jumping at her passing. Her breasts soon pushed against his thighs as her fingertips reached his shoulder blades. She could feel his thighs burning on her breasts as her hands slid down until they slid along his outer thighs.

Lilly's palms cracked against Mr. Taws's flesh. Handprints turned pink against the white roundness. She scraped her fingertips down the flesh until they met between his legs. White trails slowly turned pink to mark her hands passage. Mr. Taws moaned as Lilly dragged her fingers down the soft, hairy skin. She pulled on the weighted lumps that pulled the skin sacks downward, stretching the skin as he whimpered. Lilly smiled as she noticed him harden at her touch. Her fingertips slid off the round baubles and she seized the hardening shaft. Her nails caught on the underside of the mushroom and scraped along the soft flesh.

Mr. Taws was whimpering steadily now. His breath came in hiccups between the bleating. His legs shifted and his hips ground against the wooden table. Lilly smiled. She could feel her own flesh swelling as her spread legs pulled the heavy portal wide. Her hands slid down through the moistness to play amongst the folds, growing slick as her body reacted to her desire.

The crack of palms against flesh left a wet streak on his skin. Lilly dug her fingers into the soft, pliable flesh. One hand slid down between his legs, while the other began to beat a rhythm against his rounds. Crack, crack, crack. His flesh flexed beneath the impacts. His hips slid from side to side, bucking beneath the punishing palms. Her fingertips dragged down the crinkled skin to seize the hard shaft. Bending the hardness back until the sack draped over it, Lilly began to strip her hand up and down the hot silken rod. Up and down, dragging the skin over the mushroom head, then back down pushing the roll of skin until it gathered at the base. And all the while, her hand kept the time with cracks upon his backside. First one side and then the other turned pink.

Soon enough the stinging of her palm turned into a burning. Skin burned up her arms and into her shoulders. Her torrid skin set fuses alight along her nerves. Fuses that burned straight to the center of sensation between her legs. One hand pounded a rhythm while the other bounced in time. Then she switched. Her other hand cracking against his skin while its opposite slid along his hardness. Soon her own hips began to shift and weave. They bounced in time to the drumming of her palms and the lyrics of Mr. Taws's moans and grunts. Soon her own moans joined in chorus. Her hands bounced in time, faster and faster, drawing whimpers from his chest.

Mr. Taws screamed as he erupted. His head flung upwards. His back seized and the muscles of his strong thighs shook. His hard shaft flexed and tore itself from Lilly's hands. Great gobs of cream spewed out to collect in a pool of white on the black marble. Lilly stroked heated trails along his thighs. Her other hand squeezed and milked the hanging fruit, drawing the white cream to drip in great drops onto the floor. A quick flash of thanks that the rugs didn't extend beneath the table sped through Lilly's mind. A shake of her head drove such silly thoughts away to flitter and die in the aether.

"You've made quite a mess I'm afraid. You shall have to clean it up. But first, there is a better use for your tongue."

Lilly dragged herself up along Mr. Taws's legs. Her soft breasts crushed against his hard muscles. The hard caps on her softness scraped along his skin sending bursts of lightning through both their bodies. Lilly fought with the silk for a moment and then the blouse flew backwards, discarded and forgotten on the rich, reds and maroons of the Turkish rugs.

She seized Mr. Taws's hair and dragged his head back, bending his neck until he moaned. A bounce and a heavy thunk placed her astride the table. She slid forward, her cheeks catching on the highly polished wood. The wood sticking to her skin as if to prevent a final indignity. But she was determined. Her hips bounced along his arms and slid under her target. Her hips flexed one last time, a final adjustment, and she dropped the head into her lap. Her palm clasped him to her center as she leaned back and thrust her hips upward.

Lilly screamed as she felt the wet, hot flesh of his tongue slide along her core. It teased amongst her folds and slid upwards in the heat. Upwards until it found the hidden bud sheltering amongst the curl of flesh. Over and around the tongue bruised at the hard nob of flesh. Pounding and stroking. Teasing and flicking, his tongue assaulted her sensitive flesh. Bursts of lightning shuddered up her body, to burn out in clouds of fire in her lungs. Pain burst from her chest as already swollen flesh hardened still further. Lilly's head flicked back and forth, crushing her cheeks against the hard wooden table. Her hips bounced, seeking to drive the sensations further into her pussy. Seeking to drive the sweet torture away from sensitive flesh. Seeking to spread the sweet fires over the whole demanding region of her body.

Lilly screamed and pulled Mr. Taws's head into her, as if she could swallow him deep into her. As if she could keep him deep in her hollows, there to protect and shelter him, bringing him out only to drive her body to unimaginable heights. Her body rippled and bucked as she thrashed out her orgasm. Tears flowed from beneath eyelids as the tremors died and she lay panting on the table.

The slow withdrawing of arms from beneath her disturbed Lilly and she moaned. Cold breezes flowed over her wetness and slid up her stomach and chest. Eyes closed, she rolled onto one side, her arms between her legs, clutching at the source of her overwhelm. She lay so for a moment, unwilling to move or even to open her eyes. Her face flickered as fears burned across her exhausted brain. How would Mr. Taws feel at her boldness? Would he forgive her? Would he fire her? Oh, how could she have been so foolish? What if he fired her? What if his fragile male ego couldn't deal with her desire to trade places? Her eyes scrunched and a burst of liquid squeezed beneath the lids to trickle down her cheek.

Lilly could feel Mr. Taws's presence leave and a wave of loss washed over her. She whimpered at the deprivation. But soon, she felt his presence once again approach to stand before her. Lilly knew she must react but fear froze her muscles. At the sound of a soft click, she groaned and forced her eyes to pry open. Slits of white peeked from beneath lashes that fluttered in exhaustion.

There before her knelt Mr. Taws. Nude, still hard and stretched along one leg. The heavy sack of skin hung down along the other thigh that pointed at the floor. His face was upturned to her, his hair a thicket of black and grey. A mixture of hunger and devotion painted plainly across his features. His hands were outstretched to Lilly. Pleading. Offering. On his palms was a simple box with the lid thrown back. Two slits were visible in the purple velvet lining. One was empty. In the other, gold and silver reflected and glinted from the sparkling facets cuddled in purple velvet. Two small sapphires framed the large diamond. John smiled shyly and his lips moved silently through her tears.

3. Not Your Typical Earworm

Preface

From the 1890s we now jump forward just a few years. Mankind has spread to the stars and now ... ah, you can read the story on your own. You don't really need the backstory.

That one video watching session with Toy was very productive. In more ways than one. This is the third story that had its origins in that umm "interest-building" event. Before I start sharing why that movie night was so productive (TMI, Jean. TMI), let's just say that I put together the elements space, tentacles, and swarm in as many different ways as I could think of. (I do write Erotica after all, so TMI really is way too much information in my case.)

Now, you remember why I haven't written much Tentacle Hentai? If you don't, go check the preface for Engine Room. I'll wait. Dum, dum, de, dee. Ready? Okay. I was listening to music when I was writing and one blasted song kept going round and round and round and ... yeah. I'm sure it's happened to you. Toy was just as sympathetic to my experience with an earworm as you are. He paid for his lack of empathy later, of course. But his comments merged with my reasons and viola.

The final influence was that this was shave night. (Don't ask, TMI once again). Somehow, I came up with the question of "how do astronauts shave in space?" Followed immediately with "what would astronauts do if they shaved those parts?" And the conversation just went downhill (so to speak) from there.

Anyway, that's where this story came from.

I'm still wondering. How do astronauts shave in space?

Not Your Typical Earworm

Chuckie seized the pipe and leaned her hips forward. Her back arched and she forced her breasts upward and her hips downward, stretching out the kinks in her back. Not for the first time, she thanked the Gods of Space that there was only limited gravity on the space station. It was bad enough crouching and crawling through the passageways and repair hatches in partial gravity. She could imagine what it would be like trying to do this on Earth. Well, in fact, she couldn't imagine even being able to do some of the positions the engineers asked of her on Earth. Why can't engineers design for repair? Instead, they had her floating and crouched in the most uncomfortable positions.

Chuckie looked down her body and giggled. Obviously, the engineers didn't have these big boobs in mind when they designed the ship. Or an ass the size of hers either. Their girlfriends were probably flat, shapeless bits of nothing. Or they were. Not that the one precluded the other, she thought. Chuckie rubbed absentmindedly at a large grease stain across her bare tummy right above the bush of red hair. Time to trim the forest, she thought for the tenth time as she scratched at the shock of red. With a sigh, she reached over and retrieved her grey coveralls. Bending her knees, she pushed off and floated up the corridor. She pushed both legs into the one piece covering during the flight and then pulled the stiff paper-cloth up her hips and torso as she bounced off the smooth walls.

Chuckie bounced her way up the corridors, using handholds to change direction several times, until she finally slammed into the bridge hatch. She swung on the large wheel until her feet were pressed against the floor. A heave from her shoulders twisted the wheel and the door popped open with a whoosh of air.

Chuckie slid into the black leather pilot's chair and reached out to flick at a switch. Lights on the board flickered and the speakers at the sides of the large pseudo-glass window began to spew crackles and hisses. A few more flicks of switches and Chuckie could feel herself settle more heavily into the leather cushions. She bounced up and down for a moment, her fingers tugging at the stiff cloth where it cut between the tender flesh between her legs. Her elbow banged against another switch in a well-practiced maneuver, while she tugged and prodded at the grey cloth.

Story 3 Earworm

"Warehouse 53 to Space Dock 1. Warehouse 53 to Space Dock 1. Come in Space Dock 1."

"Warehouse 53, this is Flight Coordinator. What is your status? Over."

The voice from the speakers was tinny, and muffled as if it came from a deep well, through several layers of cheesecloth jammed in the speaker's mouth. Chuckie rolled her eyes and sighed heavily.

"Bored out of my fucking mind, but you already knew that, George. When are you going to get me out of this frickin' tin can and back home? I've been here two months already. That's a month past when I was supposed to go home. Hell, even the recyclers are having problems recovering enough paper to make my clothes. I'm going to be runnin' around here in the nude soon."

"Sorry, Warehouse 53. We're still trying to get someone clear to spell you off. That Rigelan flu has knocked the whole base on its ass. Be thankful you're up there and not down here. Half my crew has been in the medbay for the last two months. We'll get to you as soon as we can. All I can suggest is that you conserve clothes for a while. But I was actually asking how you made out with the shield leak."

"Yeah, you'd like that, wouldn't you? Just so's you can hack the internal cams and get a free girlie show. Screw that. I've got the cams locked out, shithead. So forget it. No T&A show for you, asshole. And the shield leak is fixed. I don't know who the hell designed the override circuit, but I hope he rots in hell. Fuckin' thing is not only flaky as hell, but it's a real bitch to access. You'd think they didn't realize that micro-meteors play havoc with metal and air pressures. Oh yeah, speaking of fragile things, I broke into another customer shipment of realfood. I couldn't stand the 'cycler's crap anymore."

"Fuck, Chuckie. You know we have to cover the customer's losses. And watch your language. No one will ever mistake you for a lady. You talk like a friggin' stevedore and you know the bosses listen in. This is an open line."

Chuckie sniggered, "Yeah, well maybe the assholes'll get the hint and get me off this friggin' bucket of bolts. And I am a frickin' stevedore. So if I fuckin' sound like one, there's a fuckin' reason."

Story 3 Earworm

Chuckie's laugh turned into a yawn as she hit the switch that cut off George's angry reply. A glance at the chrono built into the control panel confirmed that she'd been working for 16 hours straight. Twice the official maximum limit. No wonder she was tired. She stretched, one arm reaching for the overhead and one for the deck. She dug her palms into her eye sockets and then combed her shaggy red hair with her fingertips. Her lower bush wasn't the only hair that was in need of a trim, she thought. Her regulation quarter inch landing strip was well over the two inches maximum.

"If I stay here much longer, I'll be taking a razor to my head too, out of sheer frustration if nothing else," she grumbled aloud to herself.

Chuckie stared out of the pseudo-glass portal. The lights of transports shone steadily between the winking lights of distant stars. The sunlight turned their disarticulated hulls into half tubes of bright and black linked by strings of navigation lights. The occasional flare of steering and propulsion engines lit up their hulls in reds and oranges and bursts of white steam. Around her, Chuckie could see the stubby blocks that made up Warehouse Section 5 as they orbited the distant earth. Each silver metal box had a large number painted on its side where the sun turned the metal skin to bright pinpricks of light. Chuckie knew that a matching number could be found on each of the six sides where they hid in the darkness. Tubes filled with waiting shipments spread out around them like the spines of a metal puffer fish. Fifty-three for a fully occupied small unit and as many as two hundred and fifteen for a larger unit like Warehouse 53. Giant pinatas full of valuable goods masquerading as naval mines.

Chuckie stretched and flicked off the cameras which silently observed the rest of her small empire. One by one, lights around her small empire winked off as the station went to sleep. She scratched her red buzz cut one last time and then stood carefully. Careful not to overextend the limited gravity, she delicately slid-walked to the open hatch that led into her bunkroom. It had once been a combined storage room and lavatory for the on-duty warehouse crew. When the weeklong single-crew deployment turned into a month, Chuckie had pulled one of the beds out of a proper bunkroom and welded the metal cage to the floor.

Chuckie grinned as she pulled off her overalls and tossed them into a corner. What a load of shit moving her bedroom had caused. She had thought George was going to go apoplectic when he found out.

Story 3 Earworm

But if she was going to leave the bridge unattended while she slept, she was going to be as close to the bridge as she could get. At least this way, she could leave the hatch undogged, and if anything happened, she'd be there in a few seconds.

Her grin turned into a giggle as she picked up her razor and the vacuum hose. Imagine George's reaction if he could see her now, she thought. For a moment, she debated turning the cameras back on. Finally, she decided that as fun as it would be to tease George, it wouldn't be worth turning them back off for sleep-time. They didn't really use that much power, but every little bit of recharge time was precious. After all, the solar cells weren't really intended to provide this level of power unassisted by a shuttle engine.

Chuckie unrolled her blue hygiene kit and fiddled with the straps and Velcro for a moment. Taking a white plastic tube, the razor, the vacuum hose and some cloths, she walked over to the unprotected end of her bed, plopped down as far from the edge as possible, and then spread her legs widely. One leg rested on the bed cage while the other rested on the mattress. She set the vacuum hose so the end almost touched her pussy and turned it on by the switch in the end. The soft pulling breeze sent a ripple of anticipation from her clit to her ass. She placed one of the cloths on her thigh, and the other on the cage. The soft tingling as the cloth stuck to her thigh drew a soft moan from her. Chuckie's nipples hardened as she squeezed cream from a white tube unto her hand. The ritual had begun and her body knew the pattern well. Chuckie's hips rolled and flexed in anticipation.

The blue cream foamed as Chuckie rubbed it over her groin and down between her legs. Sticking the plastic tube against the metal cage, she flicked the guard off the razor and began to stroke the cold plasti-metal over her groin. At first, she drew the blade along her mound, carefully wiping the hair and foam onto the cloth on her leg at the end of each long stroke. The blade tickled and caressed as the flat area was bared. When she finished clearing the main bush, she rubbed her free hand over the now clean skin. Chuckie moaned at the feel of her fingers on the hypersensitive flesh. A few last bits of stubble soon fell to the sharp metal edge. Chuckie ran her hand over the now bare flesh once as if to declare the area cleared.

The remaining portions were both the most difficult and the most rewarding. Chuckie pulled on her lips stretching the skin of her labia. Chuckie shivered at the feel of fingers and metal on the sensitive flesh.

Story 3 Earworm

Short quick strokes of the blade tickled along the edges of her cleft. One direction then another then yet another, seeking out the grain of her covering. Trimming the brush as close to the root as she could cleave.

Far too quickly one side was finished. Chuckie rubbed the soft skin seeking out any wayward prickles. She told herself she was just being sure. But her fingers lingered for several minutes and her skin rippled in response. Hypersensitive flesh meeting soft fingertips. A bolt of fire and electricity flashed to circle her clit. Chuckie moaned as she switched to the other side. Soon it too was bared. Both her hands slid over the soft, bare flesh. Framing the cleft, she moaned at the feel of soft flesh. Ripples of desire burned her around her mons.

With a whimper, Chuckie slid her fingers into the valley. The tips slid over the walls of her cleft, drawing moisture from the spongy flesh. Drawing flashes of lightning from her lips. Pulling and stretching the flesh, her fingertips sought out the strands of hair. The blade slipped along the soft moist flesh eradicating each discovered tress. A frisson of fear slid along Chuckie's spine at each stroke of the sharpness so close to the blood filled tenderness. Cold metal slid over thin membranes. Fear warred with pleasure.

The sticky cloth pulled at her bare skin, sending bursts of cold fire and hot desire along Chuckie's cleft. The sensations tumbled and churned along the now wet valley. Chuckie bounced, her spine rattling the post. The cloths forgotten, striking the recycler chute only through long practice. The razor followed by habits long established. Chuckie slid her fingertips along the soft skin of her outer lips and then dipped them into the wetness of her cleft.

Chuckie's palm massaged the soft skin of her mound while her fingers slid up and down the inner lips. Her fingertips played with the folded skin, twisting and stroking the soft wet membranes. Sliding deep into the tunnel. Stroking over the hard little bud, hiding in its hood. She rubbed along the hard snake, tracing the hardness that hid beneath her skin. She stroked the clit, driving fire up along the hidden paths until it exploded from the bud that now stood proudly from its cowl.

Faster and faster Chuckie's fingers flew. Now pushing, now stroking, now diving deep to stroke the soft flesh hidden in her tunnel. She ripped at the flesh of her crotch, loving the feel of soft bare skin against her palm. Visions of George watching her, slowly stroking his own hardness flickered through her mind. Visions of holo-stars on their knees before her, chased her visions of George. They stared at her fingers, wishing their tongues could be chasing the digits. Swirling over the sensitive flesh, twisting the soft membranes, flicking against the hard bud.

Chuckie screamed as the first of her orgasms overwhelmed her. Her head flung backwards, she screamed as wave after wave of pleasure erupted between her legs. Explosion after explosion, left her eyes unfocused and her chest heaving.

Chuckie flicked the switch on the vacuum hose off with one trembling hand. She pulled her legs off their rests and gasped as they screamed, sensations rippling up her thighs to battle with her convulsing mound. She squeezed herself under the cage and pulled the covers over her now sweating body. Blackness overwhelmed her.

* * *

The screaming child disturbed her dream. Fire leapt behind closed eyelids and the child stood before her. Red light and yellow, blurring to orange lit the boy from behind, hiding his face in shadow. The boy opened his mouth and a scream arose slowly from the deeper blackness of his mouth. Loud and louder until the screaming filled her head and drove all thoughts out her throat and nose in a long stream of black smoke.

Chuckie rolled over and prised her eyes open. Only one at first. The other eye blinked and closed, refusing to open without direct physical intervention. Spiders ran from her ears, their webs shattering as the noise of the siren slowly penetrated the haze. The omnipresent chrono over the hatch showed that she had been asleep for three hours, but Chuckie could have sworn it was only two. She blinked twice and yawned, then opened her eyes wide to the blinking red light that bathed the control room and her little bedroom.

"Fuck! It's the alarm. Shit, what now?"

Chuckie scrambled her way out of the cage that was her bed and leapt across the cabin. Her feet barely contacted the floor in the reduced gravity. Her muscular arms propelled her body through the portal and aimed the missile at the control panel. One hand on the chair and one hand grasping the handhold on the lower edge of the panel served to stop her forward lunge although the sudden change in inertia made her arm feel like it was ripping from its socket. Chuckie winced as she felt her tits fly off her chest. Their weight continued on their original path only to bounce back as skin reached its maximum, slamming into her chest with enough force to bring stars to her eyes.

Ignoring the pain, Chuckie reached out to flip switches. The screens around the panel flared as cameras around the station surged to life. Most flicked through their assigned sequence in a dance of confusion. One screen on the control panel showed a single image of the control room. The thought that George was getting his girlie-show now giggled through her sleep-fogged mind. Chuckie pushed the flare of pleasure and desire away and flicked another switch. The screen on the panel flicked to a readout in green and red showing a map of the station. One block showed red and Chuckie stabbed at it. Chuckie continued to stab at the screen as it flicked from view to view until a final screen flashed in red. "Pressure drop" and "Hull integrity compromised" flashed in red. Another symbol flashed in yellow "Shield 62%" and "Possible Breach".

Chuckie flicked the switch controlling gravity to off and then pushed herself off the panel towards the hatch leading to the station. She twisted the wheel that dogged the hatch and squeezed through. Twisting the wheel to close the hatch behind her, she placed her feet on the sides of the hatch and then pushed. The rush of air flowing over her body tickled and her nipples hardened under the light caress. Chuckie pushed off from the smooth metal walls with outstretched hands, elbows rigid, bouncing along, changing direction, pulling herself through corridors. She paused occasionally to unseal hatches and then dog them again behind her.

A red light flashed over the final hatch on her path. Chuckie slammed into the wall as she grabbed the hatch wheel. Her shoulder took the brunt of an impact that left her breasts bobbing and jiggling. Her hand slapped the emergency panel beside the hatch, quickly paging through to find the air pressure and temperature readouts.

"Thank the stars, I won't need a suit."

Chuckie pressed a button and a panel slid down with a heavy clang. Inside was a thin spacesuit. A breathing mask hung from a hook on one side of the

Story 3 Earworm

suit, and a helmet on the other. A red metal box was attached to the wall between the legs of the suit.

Chuckie knelt and fiddled with the box for a moment. She soon stood up with two packages, a plastic tube of talcum powder, and a grey cardboard box. From the box, she pulled a metal and rubber leak repair kit. Grabbing the mask, and squeezing it over her head, she played with the emergency panel for a moment, then seized the wheel on the hatch and turned it.

The hatch exploded in a burst of air as Chuckie pushed the hatch open. Dogging the hatch carefully behind her, she turned and bounced across the cabin. She winced as a half-inch egg of metal struck her shoulder. In burned into her tit as she pulled it along to the wall. Chuckie slammed into the metal shelving that lined the wall with a clatter that rang against tightly strung nerves. Her breath came in short, quick bursts that fogged the plastic mask and bounced her tits on her chest. Raising the tube of talcum she released it and watched as the soft white powder formed a funnel leading to the wall. The metal and rubber plate of the repair kit soon covered the hole, the magnetic metal making a soft clang as it locked against the metal wall. The sealant made a popping noise as she pressed the button that released the foam into the hole between space and the rubber seal.

As the noise, trailed off, Chuckie broke the sealant tube off the patch leaving the metal and rubber plate behind. The two empty tubes flew into the recycler chute without Chuckie bothering to look at either. The rattle of plastic against metal told her that her aim was true as always. Instead, she focused on the still-warm, metal egg that now caressed her nipple. She picked it out of the air in front of her and rolled it around her palm. A push of strong thighs against the metal shelving propelled her to the hatch and a twist of her body soon had her pressing buttons on the emergency panel. The hatch unsealed with only the clank of metal this time, and Chuckie slid through the hatch, her attention focused on the metal lump in her hand.

* * *

Chuckie blew a kiss at the control room camera as she flicked the switch that controlled gravity on the station. A quick glance at the chrono confirmed that she had three hours more before the day would begin. She fully intended to spend that time sleeping.

Story 3 Earworm

Grabbing an empty yogurt container, she dropped the meteor into the container with a clatter and placed it carefully on the control panel. Chuckie rubbed her breast, the nipple hard and painfully pointed. She ran her hand over her mound and moaned as waves of need burned through her groin trailing behind the firm pressure. She shook herself violently and blinked several times. Quick visions of George, his hard cock slipping between her open legs flitted over her mind's eye only to be suppressed by a violent headshake. Moving carefully, she headed for her rack and another few hours of desperately needed sleep.

* * *

Chuckie groaned. Her breasts ached and her pussy itched where her spendings had dried on the outer lips and her thighs. Her night had been filled with dreams of hard cream-filled cocks and hot, wet cunts. Of hard thick rods impaling her soft channel, stretching her and banging against her burning, swollen clit. She'd dreamt of one partner after another sucking on her nipples, drawing the hard crinkled flesh out, lips pistoning on the soft flesh of her tits. Of others licking and sucking on the hard bud at the top of her cleft. The cleft that filled with liquid desire that burned the hot, spongy flesh.

Chuckie fought to open her eyes. Her eyelids stuck together, the lashes slowly dragging apart as she blinked. She blinked once, then twice. On the third blink, she screamed and tried desperately to sit up.

A mass of long tentacles filled the control room. They surged and pulsed randomly in an ever-varying mass of blue and pink. A dozen blue tentacles filled half the hatch and ran over the deck and around the cabin. They weaved like massive snakes. Some even stood erect, their ends looking like round headless cobras dancing to an unheard flute. The protective metal cage of the bed lay crushed and discarded in a corner of the room.

Long, thin tentacles of blue flesh bound her wrists and ankles to the bed. One tentacle ended in a halo of smaller tentacles. These smaller outgrowths wrapped around Chuckie's wrist and the bed frame. They extended from her wrist to her elbow in a pulsing blue coil. A second similar tentacle with outgrowths fixed her other wrist and lower arm to the other side of the bed frame. Two tentacles fixed her ankles and calves high on the bedposts. A fifth tentacle without outgrowths wrapped around her midriff.

Story 3 Earworm

Chuckie screamed and fought to drag herself off the bed. She pulled on one arm and then twisted to pull on the other. Her muscles bulged and strained as she pulled on the unyielding masses of flesh. She twisted and bounced across the bed with no effect. In time, she collapsed, her breath coming in great gasps. Her breasts wobbled on her heaving chest. Her eyes were wild and sweat stood out in great drops on her forehead.

Chuckie lay on the bed, panting in great gulps. Her eyes were wide and she stared at one tentacle, slightly larger than the rest. It rose up from between her spread legs and weaved above her midriff. It seemed to pulse and grow as she watched it. Chuckie stared at it, fascinated as with one last pulse it split. The blue skin ripped at the tip and then peeled back to reveal the pink flesh beneath. The pink flesh pulsed and swelled, hardening and shifting before her eyes. The tip expanded and spread until it formed a smooth mushroom cap, atop a long hard pink shaft covered in irregular protrusions. The glistening pink flesh was perhaps fifteen inches long and one and a half across, with a ridge of blue flesh where the outer skin had rolled back and then fused. It cobra danced between her legs, weaving and dipping within its frame.

Two other tentacles rose up on either side of the first. Even larger than the first, they continued to swell and pulse until the ends split. Blue skin peeled away to reveal pink skin beneath that continued to pulse and swell until it too split revealing a hollow interior. A long flap of pink skin flicked outward from blue lips. The two tentacles slid up Chuckie's inner thighs and over her mound. They caught for a moment on the round bulge of her tummy. They burst past and skidded over the blue tentacle that tied her midsection to the bed. The two tentacles bounced against the underside of her breasts, sending soft woman flesh rippling outward. Chuckie's nipples hardened as the brown circles of flesh bounced on her jiggling tits. The tentacles crept slowly over the soft spongy flesh, until they reached Chuckie's nipples. Pink mouths clamped on hardening brown buds. Chuckie screamed as a flash of desire burned from breast to clit.

Two other tentacles arose beside the first. Both were much thinner than the rest of the tentacles, no more than a half inch in diameter. They too pulsed and swelled, bursting to show the pink flesh. One burst, the blue skin peeling back to reveal a thinner version of the first tentacle. The long pink shaft was perhaps two feet long but much thinner than its mentor. It danced around the first tentacle, sometimes behind and sometimes in front.

Story 3 Earworm

The second of the new tentacles, split into a miniature version of the two which attacked Chuckie's breasts. It danced for a moment between her legs then sunk to slide along her outer lips, nipping at the soft skin. The long thin flap of its tongue slid along her cleft, sending a stream of desire direct to her clit. It burned there for a moment and burst in a flash of fire and heat that streamed up her spine and out her eyes. Chuckie moaned as the fire grew too much and the need emerged in an explosion of desire. The tiny mouth slid between the mounds of her lips as it reached the fold at the top. Chuckie's moan turned into a scream as the tiny mouth attacked her clit, the tiny tongue flicking along the hard, burning rod where it hid beneath the hot flap of flesh. The tiny mouth sucked, drawing flashes of lightning from the bud it suckled on.

Chuckie whimpered as she noticed the two cock-like tentacles slide down her body. She felt the larger first. It pushed on her cunt lips, dragging the flesh inwards until the prick like end burst through to slide into her tight channel. It slid deep, deep into her, touching every nerve between her legs, bouncing off that spot inside that doubled her over with the need to release. The desire to clench so hard that anything between her legs would be crushed. The compulsion to crush orgasms from the soft membranes and the hard rod that slid along them. It drilled deep, deeper than any human male she had ever welcomed. So deep that she could feel her insides swelling as it passed. Her membranes cried as the long rod withdrew, slipping over her leaking flesh. Then back again, drilling deep. Then out again, slowly slipping out until only the very tip of the head remained within her crying pussy. Pushing in, driving hard against her body, shaking her tits with the force. Again and again, in and out, driving bursts of lightning up Chuckie's spine.

Chuckie eyes crossed and her scream silenced. Her mouth was open and her head lolled from side to side, whipped by the sensations exploding from her breasts and clit. Her chest heaved and ripples crested about the hard brown dots of her nipples.

It began with a pressure against her anus. A delicate pushing against the brown crinkled mouth that hid behind the greater pressure of the tentacle pushing deep in her pussy. A wetness around her ass, and a tiny screwing pressure that slowly stretched the tight orifice. A stretching over the tiny head and shaft, followed by the slipping pressure of a long rod pushing into her fundament. A swelling as the head of the tentacle enlarged. It scraped along her insides as the rod pushed within her and then slowly withdrew leaving a coating of mucus behind. The two pricks alternated,

Story 3 Earworm

one pushing deep into her cunt while the one in her ass withdrew. The phallus shape in her ass drilling deep into her bowels while the prick shape in her cunt slid out. Then the rod in her pussy bouncing her tits with the strength of its drilling attack on her screaming spot. The rod in her ass pushed out, scraping the massive head along her inner membranes, the two colliding with an explosion of sensation as they passed, compressing the thin walls between them.

Chuckie screamed, her body overwhelmed with sensation. Her mind filled with the fire and explosions of sensations blasting her lower body. The scream turned to gurgle as a thick blue and pink phallus pushed its way between her lips. It bounced in her mouth, scraping on her teeth, sliding on her wet tongue, and colliding against her throat.

Chuckie screamed and her body arched. Her ass pushed downwards, trapping the spurting tentacle deep inside her body. The tentacle holding her stomach to the bed burst in a spray of blue and pink flesh. Her chest heaved, twisting and ripping the tentacles off her nipples. White cream sprayed from her mouth, a rocket trail of cum behind the expelled tentacle. The tentacle between her legs doubled in size and then exploded deep inside her pussy. White cream sprayed out around the pumping blue rod. It slipped slowly out of her between the pumps until it lay between her lips, the tip on her mound. It continued to pump weakly. The first few streams of cream sprayed out and over Chuckie's tits to land on her face. Each of the pumping explosions grew weaker, the spray reaching Chuckie's tits, then her tummy until the white cream dripped out to puddle on her mound and run down her hip.

Chuckie moaned and twisted, her body continuing to buck uncontrollably in the aftermath of her orgasm. From the control room, the dull mumble of the radio echoed into the caverns of her ears and twisted into the fog of her brain.

"Flight Coordinator to Warehouse 53, come in Warehouse 53. What is your status? Your alarms are going crazy. I turned your cameras on but all I can see are stripes of blue. Chuckie! Are you all right? This is George. Chuckie? Get your fuckin' ass out of bed and talk to me!"

4. The Sex Coder

Preface

No this story isn't the fourth story from movie night. I do sometimes use inspirations from real life to give my stories their initial spark. This one came from real life (believe it or not).

Toy and I are talking about redoing our home office. We're always talking about redoing the office. One of the discussions was about these wonderful chairs that are super-ergonomic. Effectively, they are the office. You don't need anything else. Of course, they're also priced way beyond our budget. But Toy keeps hinting and I keep saying no. It's a good excuse for a session so it seems to be the current trigger.

My husband, Toy, is a programmer when he isn't serving me. He says he isn't and he keeps trying to explain what he really is but I can't understand it at all. So I tell everyone he's a programmer. All I know is he does something mysterious with computers and when I start cursing Windows, he's the one who hits a button (usually one) and gets it working again.

We're also both avid gamers. I'm better than he is. In fact, the reason he's called Toy is directly related to my beating him at his favorite game. He really shouldn't have bet me he could beat me. Silly boy. Now I get to beat him – repeatedly. Not that he minds his punishment, you understand.

Finally, as I write this, there is a discussion going on about artificial intelligence and robots. How can mankind protect itself from its own creations? Will people lose their jobs because of robots? How will we replace work when working is obsolete? What will happen to our income? That last one being far too close for comfort, of course.

In any case, the night before I wrote this story, Toy and I were talking about AI, the new work, and gaming. My mind being what it is (I write Erotica, remember), I jumped to this story. Add in the chair (it really is a nice chair), a little bit of people not reading as much, and you've got the basis of this story.

So, where do you think Erotica is going?

The Sex Coder

Megan sat back in her chair stretching one more time in a day filled with stretches. She slipped her hands beneath her red hair and arched her back. She twisted in her padded chair, her knotted spine stretching until she could look out of her cubicle into that of Teresa. Megan giggled as she noticed Teresa also stretching. A quick flash of jealousy flashed across Megan's face as she noticed that Teresa's large breasts stretched upwards. If only her girls were as large and firm as Teresa's were. Instead, they were tiny little bumps, with a capital B minus at their largest. They barely warranted a bra, which is why Megan usually passed on that dubious pleasure. Megan sighed and twisted to face the beige material of her cubicle wall. Megan groaned and closed her eyes to blot out the sight of a wall of company-approved course diplomas on bland beige card stock. Beige on beige on beige. Snoring and boring, that's corporate life. With a sigh, she dropped her arms, shook herself, and then turned to the computer screen on the desk in front of her. Megan stared at the screen for a moment, her hands poised above the black keyboard. She groaned and ground her palms into her eyes.

"Terri, help. I can't take writing about sex any more. Is it time for coffee yet?"

Teresa laughed, "At least you get to write the Troll and dungeon scenes. Yay, BDSM. A little bit of kink to break up the afternoons. I'm stuck with the wedding night and feast scenes. If I have to type 'Oh my prince, oh, oh' one more time I'm going to upchuck. Tell me one more time, why are we working as narrative writers on one more sex game and not scriptwriters on a big blockbuster?"

"Because someone promised us there would be lots of handsome IT guys with lots of money and no girlfriends. And 'cause all the movie jobs pay shit."

"Yeah, well someone lied."

"Must've been Lady Nose-up. Which reminds me, we have a meeting with Her High and Mightiness in forty-five minutes. So we'd better get a hustle on if we want a coffee."

"Oh God, let's go then, I can't take any more sex without coffee and a chocolate bar. And I certainly

Story 4 The Sex Coder

can't take another PMS fueled scream-fest without fortification. Preferably something stronger but coffee and chocolate will have to do in a pinch."

Megan laughed. She pushed her chair out and bounced up. Grabbing her purse from beside the grey screen, she skipped to catch up with Teresa.

* * *

Megan stumbled back to her desk and shook her head. What the hell did that busybody think she did all day? Writing was creative work. She couldn't just crank it out at the snap of her nonexistent fingernails. Megan's ears still rang from her boss's screaming rant.

"We've got to increase output. The coders are pumping out work fine but we're running behind. Why can't you write faster? I've known writers that could pump out twice as much work as the two of you put together. And frankly, the sex you're writing is boring. Even our coders are noticing that it's ho-hum. And they don't even know what real sex is. Hell, I'm afraid to read the customer feedback forms. They're calling it shit. And that's the nicest thing they're saying. It's a fucking turn-off. Things are so bad that we've had to cut staff in sales and testing. And you two don't want to be next."

Megan groaned. It wasn't her fault if the producer couldn't think past her crotch and decades old tropes. Hell, the whole D & D sex thing had been done to death. Yeah, it was boring. After all, how many ways could you connect a Troll and a Halfling female without splitting the female in two? And this stupid idea of a stupid chair that was somehow supposed to make her scripts sexier and her more productive was just that. Just one more stupid idea in a string of stupid ideas! As if a chair, no matter how expensive, could make her focus. She knew how to focus, damn it. She'd been doing it ever since she joined the stupid company. Megan growled and swallowed a scream. Her entire body shook in a paroxysm of anger. Looking at the clock on her computer, she reached over, and smashed at the mouse. A few angry clicks later and the file had been properly saved and the computer turned off. Megan seized her purse, and turned to go. The chair was due in tonight. So tomorrow would prove if this chair would work or if it was just one more in a long litany of stupid moves by management. But for tonight, a bottle of algae wine, some quick-nuke curry, and a classic romance novel was just what she needed.

Story 4 The Sex Coder

* * *

Megan's brow furrowed as she walked up the corridor to her desk. The office seemed more crowded this morning. The corridors seemed tighter. And she was sure that the pair of cubicles she and Teresa shared hadn't crowded the corridor last night. Maybe Dragon Lady had given them bigger offices. Yeah sure. Megan grunted and half laughed. As if that would ever happen.

Megan stopped as she reached her office. Her jaw dropped, and she stepped back to check the nameplate on the wall. Yes, that was her name. She had a door now with what appeared to be a privacy mode. Looking through the currently clear window, she recognized the certificates on the wall. The rest of the office, however, was completely unrecognizable. Opening the door and stepping in, she gazed in awe at the changes. The desk itself had been replaced with something better described as a credenza. Her favorite shade of deep purple with scarlet highlights and the occasional pop of pumpkin had replaced the beige on beige scheme of yesterday. Megan giggled. It looked more like a sexy bedroom for one of her erotic bimbo characters rather than a proper modern office. The presence of a swing chair of some sort tucked in the corner opposite the desk only emphasized the inappropriate nature of the color scheme. The large full-length mirror cemented her opinion of the color scheme.

As for the office chair sitting in the middle of the room, it looked like something out of a science fiction movie of the last century. It wasn't so much a simple chair as an all-encompassing workstation in deep purple plastic and red metal. A large metal C enclosed the workstation. It obviously included the electronics and wiring which stuck out everywhere. A helmet affair hung down from the upper arm. Various tubes circled down from the main ridge beam turning the unit into a ball shape.

In the center was the chair itself, about three feet from the floor and slightly reclined with two separate footrests. The active plastic shell was designed to mold itself to her body so no cushion was needed. However, Megan knew that an air cushion provided extra comfort while allowing the machine to self-clean for the ultimate in sanitation. A desk surrounded the chair in case the occupant needed something in the physical world. It even had a coffee cup holder built in.

Story 4 The Sex Coder

Megan whistled. That sucker had to be equipped with the very latest in AR technology. Sitting under that hood with the air pressure turned on would feel like being there. Of course, you would have to be nude to get the best use of it. Megan giggled at the thought. She had seen units like this designed for the hard-core sex-gamer but had never had the courage to try one. And she certainly didn't have the money to buy one.

Megan placed her Horny Tim's coffee cup in the cup holder (French Vanilla - double-double - extra caffeine and no aphro-chems, of course). Dazed, she walked over to the credenza and filed her purse, locking the unit with her fingerprint. A manual for the chair lay on the desk with a note that read, "Don't worry about the manual. We have a full training in the meeting room first thing. Join us." Megan shook her head, grabbed her coffee cup, and wandered off looking for the meeting room.

* * *

Megan entered her office in stunned silence. She turned and flipped the switch on the privacy door to private. For a moment, she stared at the closed door as the clear glass darkened to black. A hum began above her as the silence circuits began enclosing her in privacy. She shook her head and then began to strip. Her blue pseudo-wool and synth-silk bolero jacket was first. She slipped it over the neo-wood clothes hanger that she found on the wall beside the door. Her long blue pseudo-wool pencil skirt was next. It fit under the jacket on clips. Megan stood for a moment staring at the hanger and her clothes. Her bare legs felt odd beneath her. The flaps of her synth-silk blouse tickled the tops of her thighs. Goose bumps ran up and down her hips and thighs. She bit her lip and stared at her legs. Strangers below her, holding her up by some queer magic in defiance of the laws of nature. Her head swam and her sight went black for a moment.

Megan shook her head and her hands moved of their own accord to begin pulling at the quasi-pearl buttons of her blouse. They popped one by one until she worked her way down to the last button holding the two sides of the blouse together over her blue panty covered mound. She blinked and bit her lip, and with a last effort undid the final button. The slippery blouse slid down her arms and Megan stood there for a moment feeling the chill of the room on her hardening nipples. She reached over and slid the blouse onto the last of the clothes hangers with a shiver. As she turned from hanging her blouse, she spotted her reflection in

Story 4 The Sex Coder

the mirrored wall. Tiny and trim or so she thought the men described her. Although, personally, she felt her thighs were a little too thick and her currently naked breasts just a little too small. Her fingers picked at the blue lace panties in the mirror, reluctant to show everything. But with a final sigh, her eyes never leaving the mirror, she slipped the band of blue down her hips and watched as the lace slid down her legs.

Megan rubbed her hand over her mound and plumped her breasts one more time. Then she turned and climbed into the chair. As she climbed up the air cushion began to pump supporting air around her. Twisting until she was comfortable, she pulled the eye shield and headset down until it covered her face. Goose bumps ran up her back as the cool air slid beneath her. Megan reached out with one hand and flicked on the computer by a switch on her chair. Her other hand reached out to pick up her cup of coffee. Megan jumped as her returning cup passed through a keyboard that appeared suddenly in the air before her. A large screen appeared above her chair. She reached out with her free hand and swatted at the empty air as the computer reacted to her keyboard presses and mouse clicks. Megan took a sip of her coffee and settled back to work.

Megan was busy writing the script for yet another encounter between a Troll and a female Halfling when Teresa buzzed her. Her avatar appeared in the doorway as Megan pressed the answer button. It shimmered as it appeared and Megan giggled. The avatar was dressed in a flowing white princess gown and Teresa's normally black hair was purple with pink and green stripes. Her normally tiny waist was half its real size and her normally abundant breasts were absolutely immense. They bounced uncontrollably as the avatar twirled.

"Hey, slowpoke. You haven't changed your avatar yet. Haven't you figured out how yet? I found the customization tab and it's a knees-up. What do you think? Should I keep it? Or go for the barbarian or maybe the nudist look? Better not do the nudist, it might give people a heart attack."

"No, I don't think that would be a good. Not exactly business-like."

"I'll bet you haven't even tried out the extras yet?"

Story 4 The Sex Coder

"Not yet. I've been writing and I was afraid they'd distract me. Maybe after coffee break? I'm dying to find out what you think about being nude in the office. I think this is going to take a bit of getting used to."

"Oh, you fuddy-duddy. It's kind of naughty. And the extras are fantastic. You have to try them. But coffee first sounds great. Give me a minute to get dressed and I'll knock on your door for real."

* * *

Megan entered her office, undressed and climbed back into her chair. She stared at the script she had just written and hummed to herself. It was good but it still just didn't seem to have that passion. Megan sighed and decided to explore the extras options on her chair before editing the script for a fifth time. The options on the extras tab were interesting and Megan got lost for a moment in exploring the alternatives. Her mind flitted down odd hallways as she read some of the titles: Machine pound, Vibratory delight, Shake a clit, Man between. Finally, her eyes spotted Slow & Hot Real-Tongue and her fingers pounced on the button. Megan hesitated for a moment as a long list of choices appeared. With a muttered "Oh, what the Hell," she jabbed at the random choice button. A red band appeared across the top of her virtual display, "Working. Please return to work. Your request is being arranged and will start momentarily." Megan crinkled her forehead at the odd message. She shook her head in puzzlement. Deciding to ignore the odd phrasing, she grinned and went back to her editing.

Megan was busily rewriting a scene between the heroine, the hero, and a troll for the fifth time, when a buzzing snuck between the strains of Mozart she was listening to. The troll stopped pounding his massive cock into the hero, the heroine stopped grinding her ass into the troll's face, and even the softly waving grass below Megan froze as her fingers came away from the keyboard. The red bar flashed to green, the words on the bar changed to 'Starting program', and Megan felt the chair begin to readjust. Her invisible legs spread and bent as the footrests ground to the side and then pushed in. She gasped as she felt herself slide down the chair and a cool breeze slide over her now widely spread pussy. She glanced down but the chair was in full disembodiment mode. She couldn't actually see her body but she knew that anyone not hooked into the headset would have had a view deep into her body. Her pussy clenched at the thought of her exposure.

Story 4 The Sex Coder

Megan shrugged her shoulders and returned to the scene. The three avatars bounced around her as they sought their pleasure. Megan groaned at her creations and then gasped as she felt a soft wet touch slide along her perineum, tease along the soft tissues of her inner lips, and then slip around the hood. She swore as the wet thing tickled the hood of her clit and then traced along the ridge of buried reactivity, sending flashes of sensation exploding from her hardening bud. Megan bucked as explosions fired between her legs. She moaned as her fingers sought out a particularly boring piece of text and began to type. The troll avatar's tongue grew longer and thinner. It flickered deeper into the heroine's body. Drilling deep into her vagina, it tickled the ridges and pounded on the girl's walls. The girl gasped and twisted, moaning as the sensations vibrated through her body. Megan gasped as the tongue between her own legs found the hard bud and began to flick against her center. It dug between the folds and slipped along the wet flesh.

Megan clutched at the virtual keyboard as the tongue between her legs tickled downwards, twisting the soft flaps, and playing amongst the folds. She gasped as the thing slipped into her tunnel, flicking over her ridges and sucking juices from her body. She shook for a few moments and then, with a groan that shook her all the way to her toes, she began to type quickly. Around her, the avatars groaned and twisted.

Megan felt her stomach heave as the sensations exploded through her pussy. They burned her thighs and rippled her mound. Liquid need spilled from her to trickle down her ass cheeks. Around her disembodied form, the avatars were frantic now. The troll pounded deep into the bowels of the hero. His tongue slithered over the heroine's cunt, flicking at the now massive clit. The hero clutched at his massive cock, pounding at its hardness, the purple head jumping in his hands as the enormous cock behind him rammed deep into his bowels.

Megan sighed as the tongue found a particularly sensitive spot. The hot, wet probe dug deep into her body and pulled at the ridged flesh that lined her vagina. It flicked over the walls, sucking out the sweet wetness it found there. Megan's hips flexed and her pussy clenched. She could feel her clit swelling and the burning buildup of lust beneath her mound. Megan moaned.

On the screen, the Pretty Princess suddenly changed from a meek, little thing passively laying back

Story 4 The Sex Coder

while being pounded by the Troll, into a raging berserker. She kneed the Troll and pushed it off. Jumping to her feet, she slapped the Troll's face and seized the dildo shaped cat'o'nine-tails from the Troll's belt. She swung the black leather straps against the whimpering creature until it lay in a cringing heap at her feet. Then, seizing its greasy head, she forced the chin and nose between her legs and clamped down as Megan's hands flew over the keyboard.

Megan groaned as the tongue slipped out of her cavern and tickled along the folds that led to her clit. It played over the hard bud, flicking at the hood, and pushing against the hard ridge of sensitivity. Megan's tits shook. The now hard nobs bounced as wave after wave of lust burst up her spine to explode in flares of fire behind her eyelids. She gasped at the sensations attacking her groin. Her clit felt like a balloon swollen to ten times its size. She could feel the liquid lust gathering between her legs, and dripping down her ass cheeks.

The Pretty Princess pushed the Troll away from her. Her foot flashed as she kicked the creature in the balls. Grinning with an evil gleam, she dived on the poor creature and seized its rock-hard prick in her hand. Her other hand grabbed his balls and dragged the hard lumps away from his body until his soft skin was stretched like the head of a drum. The hand on his prick began to strip slowly up and down the hard rod. Her teeth flashed as she bit down on the soft bulbous mushroom head. Megan's hands stabbed at the keys, every pounding motion overwhelmed with anger and building lust.

Megan groaned as the tongue between her legs lashed at the hard nob that erupted from her cleft. The tongue smashed against the hard flesh, driving explosions of almost pain from her burning clit. Explosions of fire and heat that bounced from cunt to mound and mound to cunt until it erupted along her spine, quivering her tummy and shaking her tits. Megan grabbed at one nipple and pulled hard, stretching the crinkled brown flesh atop the soft white mound. Stretching it and sucking in the joyful pain, mixing pain and pleasure into a sweet brew that threatened to erupt through her spine and blow out through her ears.

The Pretty Princess chewed her way down the Troll's massive cock. Her head bounced as she sucked the hard rod. Her teeth caught in the soft skin, dragging it behind her, leaving white streaks that turned pink and angry. The Troll's head whipped back and forth as the

Story 4 The Sex Coder

woman assaulted his rigid member. Tears ran down his cheeks as desire built within his swelling balls.

Megan's hand flew over the keyboard, pounding the air in her excitement. Her other hand tugged and palpitated her breast. She pulled on the hard, brown nob stretching it out and then releasing it. Her hand slapped the soft tit and her fingers dug deep into the soft mound, milking desire from her breast until it ran in burning trails down her stomach to gather in flaming pools around the tongue flicking at her throbbing clit.

Megan groaned and whimpered. Her tongue lolled from between swollen lips as her eyes flickered shut. Her fingers continued to pound at the keyboard as her hips twisted and rolled with every flick of the hot, wet tongue. The Pretty Princess was smacking the heavy flesh now, her head bouncing down the stiff rod. Her hand flashed as a crack split the air. Her teeth gnawed at the purple head as crack after crack rattled up the hard shaft. Her other hand grasped the heavy balls, pulling and twisting on them as her mouth slipped down the dark red shaft. Her hand smacked at the Troll's thick thighs and then began to pound a rhythm on the thick swelling of balls twisted in their now thinly spread sheath of skin. The Troll screamed around the thick cock the hero pounded into its mouth. White bubbles of froth dribbled down its cheeks around the pounding rod. The Pretty Princess laughed around her own gagging rod, her teeth cutting at the soft skin of the Troll's cock as she laughed. Her throat rippled around the large mushroom head. The Troll's eyes rolled upwards to gaze into his forehead.

Megan's tits were shaking now, bouncing on her heaving chest. The nipples swung wildly, each shudder burning a flare of desire down through her spine to her stomach and below. She screamed as the tongue between her legs smashed against her clit. Lips sucked the fold of flesh, deep into a hot, wet cavern. Teeth scraped over sensitive flesh, wet flesh flickered over sensitive nerve endings. Megan could feel her stomach heave. The swelling between her legs increasing and growing almost unbearable now. The urge to release the fluids that filled her center turned insistent. The desires that wracked her lower body screaming for release. Megan whimpered in her need to have something, anything fill the swollen emptiness between her legs. The image of a hard cock pounding into her soft flesh burned through her mind, blinding her to the scenes that swirled in the AI helmet.

The Pretty Princess now sat astride the Troll. Her hips bounced with every flex of her thighs, forcing the angry hardness deep into her center. It disappeared into her soft cunt only to reappear moments later, angry and wet and red. And then it vanished in soft pink flesh and blonde curls. Her ass shook as she smashed against the Troll's massive thighs. The girl's tits bounced as she fucked the Troll. Her nipples slapped at the hero's thighs as he stood before her, legs spread, his hands on his hips. His head was forward, and moans rippled up his chest. Her head swung with every bounce of her hips, forcing her lips over his hard shaft. Her fingers clasped at his swinging balls as her lips tripped over the ridges of his cock. Fingernails scraped along soft skin, leaving trails of pink, burning pleasure.

Megan's head twisted and shook as wave after wave of release pounded through her body. Her spine arched and she twisted and weaved against the air-cushioned chair. Her hips heaved forcing the flicking tongue against the sensitive flesh and then fleeing as the sensations overwhelmed her painfully sensitive flesh. Wetness sprayed along her thighs as her clenching flesh squeezed lubricants in a fine spray that misted the tongue licking her pussy lips and down her thighs.

Megan screamed as the sensations tumbled through her. Her body shook as the swollen flesh burst in an explosion of fire and light that echoed through her synapses. It left her quaking and bouncing against the chair. Her fingers shook as she weakly stabbed at the keyboard.

In the helmet, the Pretty Princess exploded in a release of passion that matched Megan's own. Her back arched and her tits bounced as the hero released between her lips. White streams of cum spiked out and exploded against her cheeks and forehead. It tricked down her chin and splashed into her hair. Beneath her, the Troll arched its back. The Pretty Princess was flung high as explosions of cum from his massive pipe pushed her upwards, twirling her on his mushroom head until with a cry of ecstasy fulfilled she slid down his rod. She collapsed to lay on his legs, the massive rod bent downwards, and a stream of white cream spreading outwards over the creature's belly.

Megan collapsed against the chair. Her hips jerked uncontrollably. She tore the helmet off and let it hang against her heaving chest. Her eyes were unfocused and her hair hung in sweaty ropes. Slowly the room swam into focus.

Story 4 The Sex Coder

Beneath her, the chair groaned and shifted. The sound of air seals releasing and pneumatics pumping filled the room. It banged against her eardrums and jangled against the screech of metal on metal. Megan twisted a head that had grown some hundred pounds in the last hour until she could barely see the area between her thighs. Her chest heaved with the effort, obscuring her vision. Between her legs, a drawer slid open revealing a bearded face. A body slowly appeared behind it and soon, a male was scrambling to his feet before her. His pants were tented painfully before him and his hands seemed to fly uncontrollably around his hips.

Megan's hands twisted and slapped at the air, as they proved too heavy to lift, leaving her body open and unprotected to the view of her co-worker. Aftershocks pounded through her body leaving her stomach heaving and her chest shaking. Slowly Megan's eyes focused on the man's face. Recognition slowly spread over her face as she stared at the adoring visage.

"God, Megan. That was wonderful. I've always wanted to ask you out but I was afraid you'd say no. I mean, I know I'm the shift supervisor and all, but I'm still just a programmer and you ... you're the writer.

You're the one with the wonderful brain for sex. You think up all the situations and stuff. And me, I'm nobody. And besides, you're fucking gorgeous and I'm just a geek. You'd never go out with me. Oh God, not in a million years. But when I got the call ... You'd actually called on me to help you. I didn't think. I mean, you could have anyone. We'd all love for a chance to help you write. I mean, who wouldn't? But when you picked me, oh fuck. I hope I was good enough for you. I tried. I really did. Please give me another chance. Please. You taste so wonderful."

"Jamie, shut up. Give me a moment to get my breath back. Oh, and drop those pants. I have another chapter to write before lunch. I need some more inspiration and you look like you've got just the thing I need."

5. The Barn

Preface

Traditionally, I've finished the last story in this collection with a taste of my latest (or next) book on Amazon. Unfortunately, I'm releasing this book as soon as I finish Well Met in Dragon Light which I already previewed in Steamy Shorts 4. I haven't decided what my next book is, so I don't have a first chapter I can share. But since this is the last book in the series, I really didn't want to break this self-imposed rule. What to do?

I do have another book I can use and interestingly enough it actually is my latest. It's just not available on Amazon. Which is good for you. So, here's the first chapter of my latest book, The Barn.

Why is this good for you? Want more of this book? It is available. And the real good news is that it is free. All you have to do is go websurfing to https://jeanecrivain.wordpress.com/newsletter/ and sign up for my newsletter. You'll get a copy of this book, advance notice of other books I'm publishing, advanced notices about promotions, a chance to get free books, and much, much, more.

How can you beat that deal?

Okay, so where did this book come from? In Steamy Shorts 4, I wrote The Hen Party. It was a story about Lady Margaret, who lived in an England where all the males (and some females) had been exposed to the Desire Virus. The result of the disease was that half the human race became incapable of thinking above their waists. (Sounds like real life, doesn't it?) Males had come to be treated as animals as a result. The Hen Party was supposed to be a short story. But it ended up a novella.

The story went on forever, however, I really loved the characters, and the world I had created. Like the world of Queen Bee in Steamy Shorts 1, I couldn't get the world out of my head. I had to write another story (or two or three) in that world. So when I decided to write a book to give to my loyal fans, I set it in the world of Lady Margaret. It was either that or a space opera.

Story 5 The Barn

Now, part of the reason I loved the story was that there were two questions that were still rattling around my head after The Hen Party. Firstly, if men were treated like prize horses, where would they be kept? That gave me the title and the basic setting. Secondly, if males were that subservient, how would women ensure the race continues? Before you put yourself too far into the gutter, I'm referring to all the other little things that lead up to the bedroom. Add to that a news item on breeding prize horses and I had my story.

So enjoy. As for me, I'm going to go spend some time with my own prize stud. Oh, Toy ... I'm finished working ...

The Barn

Margaret, Seventh Duchess of Redhill, slowly pulled on her grey gloves. The leather was soft and supple as it slid tightly over her tiny hand. She tugged the long cuffs up her arms, enjoying the gentle pull of the sticky leather on the delicate hairs and skin. She patted the fine leather where it met her elbow, enjoying the softness. Sliding the fingers of her bare right hand between the gloved fingers of her left hand, she pushed on the quirks until the glove hugged her fingers perfectly. Running her hand along her left arm she pushed and prodded at the leather until the glove sat precisely as it should. A second leather glove slid over her right hand and she repeated the process until both gloves hugged her arms tightly.

Looking down at her gloved hands, Margaret hummed in pleasure. She reached up and plumped her breasts where they sat on the heavy, black leather underbust corset. Her fingers flicked at the brown nipples enjoying the quick flare of sensation that zigzagged to her clit as leather scraped on crinkled skin. She smiled as she stared at her reflection in the mirror of the large hall tree. Her long grey skirt was rolled in front to display her long legs clad in black stockings and her white frilly pantalets. Tall grey leather boots with high brass stiletto heels reached to her knees, the black lacing tied in a bow at the top. A red ribbon tied in a bow held the two halves of the white pantalets together. The bow was perfectly centered over her visible mound, emphasizing rather than hiding the soft entrance below.

Margaret continued to stare at her reflection as the tall, nude male behind her draped a matching grey cape over her shoulders. The soft fur lining tickled her bare back and Margaret sighed in pleasure at the sensation. She reached up and gave the cape a final adjustment and then turned to the male. She stared into his sad eyes for a moment. Her eyes flicked over the thick black leather collar that held his head erect. They slid down over his muscular chest and past his well-defined stomach to the stiff rod that poked out from his groin. One hand reached out to cup his balls. She pulled on the soft bags until the skin was taut. His hard nuts swelled clearly against her thumb and forefinger. The crack of her hand on his prick rang against her ears. Her hand slashed downwards again and again, cracking across the hard rod. It bounced downwards, bouncing off her hand and then bouncing up until it almost struck his stomach with each blow. It hung quivering as the male gripped at his thighs. His face grimaced and he whined.

Story 5 The Barn

Margaret grasped his hard prick and slowly stripped up and down. Her hand squeezed tightly on the hard shaft, and then crushed the soft purple head. With a giggle, she slapped his hard prick again and pulled on his balls until he fell to his knees at her feet. She lightly slapped his face and then looked up as a cough echoed in the anteroom.

"I believe your rickshaw is here, Your Grace. The breeding barn has been warned to expect you. I was told that the stable mistress, herself, will be waiting to assist you. Will you be wanting tea when you return?"

"I'm not certain. Tea is unlikely, and I rather doubt that I shall be back before supper in fact. Perhaps it would be best if I eat at the club. I do believe that I will be hungry afterward. Oh, do have a chilled demi of my champagne waiting in my room for when I do return. Also please have a service beast prepared and in my room. I rather doubt that the breeding beasts will be up to my standards."

"Very well, Your Grace. I'll see to it personally. Enjoy your day."

Margaret's butler bowed deeply as she opened the door and passed a large grey handbag to her mistress. The butler's bare breasts swung freely beneath the black frock coat. As Margaret swept out the door, the butler turned and clipped a leash to the male's collar. With a tug on the leash, the butler forced the kneeling male to bury his head between her legs as she swung the door closed with a heavy thump.

Margaret smiled as her heels clicked on the cobblestones. The rickshaw was a long distance hire. Unlike most of its kind, it had only a single nude male in front and room for just two passengers in its leather-upholstered carriage. The driver normally sat behind the passengers in a covered frame. For the moment, however, she stood beside a set of stairs placed to assist entrance to the cab.

"How excellent. Is this a real Han'som' carriage? But not your typical one, I notice. And I note that you only have one male."

"Yes, mum. Specially built for me by Josephine Hansom, herself, it was. For the long runs. Light, quick to maneuver and easy to pull, just like I asked. And Jack here, he don't need no others helping him or

Story 5 The Barn

spelling him. No matter how far he has to run. He's been specially trained by meself, he has. Gots wha' you call stamina, he has, has my Jackie. Gots a nice big package too for when the bumpin' gets ta be too much, if'n you know what I mean.

"But we'd best be gettin' on. It's several hours to get there, it is. We'll be takin' to the back roads, if'n it please your ladyship. Tha' way we won't have to deal wi' no steam 'shaws. Foul smelly things like to shake themselves loose on the cobbles, they do. You just tuck yourself in there, and we'll be off, we will."

Margaret smiled tolerantly and settled herself into the well-padded leather as the driver retrieved the steps and climbed into her seat in the covered frame behind the passengers. The warm leather cupped her back as Margaret stared at the back of the nude male. His hair was long, and hung in a braid almost to his fine ass. His shoulders were wide with bulbous deltoids. His back was well defined and muscular. The bumps of his spine were clearly visible where they ran down to the large half-globes of his ass. His cheeks were round and would have been quite pleasant to grip were it not for the flat sides. Margaret licked her lips at the sight of his heavy balls swinging between his muscular thighs. This was going to be a pleasant trip. Jack was going to be quite a pleasant view. She smiled and then sniffed at the thought of calling a male by a name. "How old fashioned," she giggled.

* * *

Margaret looked up from her book as the Han'som' pulled up to the white clapboard and grey fieldstone stables. She had spent the first hour or so of the trip admiring the mount pulling the rickshaw. She loved the way the muscles of his back strained to pull the cab when it caught on the rough cobbles. And the way his gluteus maximus shifted as he ran. The way his balls swung as he ran had also deserved close study. But even the occasional glimpse of his prick head bouncing into view was not enough to keep her focus for long. As boredom set in, Margaret had pulled a thin volume from her purse and turned to reading. Delicious words from the Marquise De Sade always helped to pass the time in piquant contemplation.

Margaret placed the thin red volume back in her grey handbag and looked around as the rickshaw bounced to a stop. It rocked back and forth unsteadily for a moment. Margaret smiled at what appeared at first glance to be a well-kept country stables. The

Story 5 The Barn

cobblestone lane leading to the stables was lined with old willow trees that draped their heavy leaf-laden limbs over the lane. Beyond the trees, Margaret could see large paddocks of well-trimmed grass. A double storied grey fieldstone manor house in the Tudor style stood a little way off from the stables on its own laneway. Four white clapboard and grey fieldstone stables faced the lane. White wooden fences blocked out a paddock between and behind the stables.

The stable mistress stood before the nearest of the stables. She was tall and strongly built rather than delicate. Her black hair stood out against her white coat and riding breeches. Her hands were clasped behind her back and she stood at ease waiting for her guest. Several young women in corduroys and rough cotton shirtsleeves peeked out from the shadows. As Margaret climbed down the steps to stand weaving beside the rickshaw, the stable mistress tugged on a wisp of hair hanging down over her forehead.

"Good day, Your Grace. Welcome to Maidenhead Stables. I assume you will be keeping your driver engaged until your return? Good. Jean here will show her to a stall where she can clean up her mount, have a bite to eat, and relax until you are finished.

"In the meantime, we have selected four good mounts for you. All are of superior breeding stock, and all have pedigrees with clear royal or noble ties. As for the female breeding surrogates, we have selected two. Again, both have pedigrees with clear royal or noble ties. Additionally, both sets of breeding stock have produced a good selection of Desire Virus resistant siblings. Unfortunately, as you are aware the Desire Virus attacks all males and a percentage of the females leaving neither capable of advanced thought or indeed anything much beyond a focus on reproduction. In addition to their high status, these particular breeders come from families that have produced well over the usual seventy percent of resistant females. Having said that, please do remember that while Maidenhead Stables does its utmost to ensure a successful foaling, we cannot guarantee your child will be Desire Virus free. I presume the office has discussed with you the alternatives should a child be born infected. Good. Now, I understand that you wish to participate? It is unusual but not unheard of. We really don't recommend it. What form of protection will you want to use?"

"Nothing at all, thank you. In fact, my physician has assured me that I will be at my most fertile today. While I have accepted your requirement to use surrogates, I am hoping that I will become pregnant."

Story 5 The Barn

"Indeed? Now that is very unusual. Most of our clients find the surrogate process much more convenient and infinitely safer. You do realize that these are not your normal house males. They are breeders not pets. The Desire Virus has affected them rather strongly and somewhat differently than your usual pet. Not only are they fertile but they have lost any ability to think beyond fuck and feed. Left to their own devices they would fuck until they died of exhaustion. Very few resistant women can survive an encounter with them. That's why grooms are always in multiples."

"Yes, I am very aware of the difference between house pets and breeders. My mother was quite famous for her stables."

"We really do recommend against it. There are safer if less pleasant methods. However, if that is your wish, let me show you to our breeding facility. Everything has been arranged as per your request. If there is anything else either I or my staff can do for you, please do not hesitate to ask."

"You have quite a large farm, I see."

"Yes, we are quite proud of our stables. One of the buildings is given over to simple milking. We have processing facilities for both female milk and male cream hidden behind the building at the far end. We're quite proud of the quality of the cream produced. The rest of the stalls are split between foaling breeders, and breeders awaiting servicing. We also have a small area for training both males and females. However, that is done in a separate part of the farm so as to avoid disturbing the breeders. I can show you later if you wish."

Margaret thanked the stable mistress as they entered the nearest of the stables. Margaret took a deep breath, fully expecting to smell the musky scent of old sex. She smiled as her nose detected the gentle sweet tang of lavender. The stable mistress guided her charge into the large building, past several offices and a hallway. Almost at the end of the building, the stable mistress unsealed a door and stood aside to allow her guest to enter first.

The room was spacious almost to the point of being oppressively so. What saved it was that it had been broken into a number of separate areas through the placement of furniture. As she entered, a seating area in high Victorian style spread before her. In the

Story 5 The Barn

corner to her left, a delicate bedroom in lace, with cream coverings and dark brown wood centered around the largest bed, Margaret had ever seen. Beyond the Victorian sitting room, was what Margaret had described as a playroom. Stocks and a St. Andrews cross dominated that area. Finally, a large wooden tub sat in the last corner. Wisps of white steam trickled off its surface.

Margaret smiled. Her pleasure at the room was evident in the light that shone from her eyes and cheeks. She looked around, oohing and ahhing at each new sight. Turning carefully, she seized the stable mistress's hand and thanked her profusely. All that remained was to introduce the breeders. Margaret bit her thumb and stamped her feet in pleasure.

The stable mistress smiled and shook her black hair. She guided Margaret to the back of the breeding room. Margaret smiled widely as she noticed the four males chained to the wall of the playroom. In front of furthest wall, was a rough table in wood blackened by time. On the table was a selection of toys, ranging from a leather bullwhip to a delicate crop, from a tiny steam driven vibrating probe to a dildo as large as Margaret's arm. Margaret licked her lips as she picked up a silver ball weight and bounced it on her palm.

"Shall I introduce you to our selection? This fine stud is M60A1010. We call him Ten for short. His father was a scion of the royal court. As you can see, he is quite large. He has produced almost three dozen Desire Virus resistant children at this point for a number of noble families.

"If you prefer blondes, this fine specimen is M59B1720. Twenty is a former member of the German Royal harem. We were fortunate in obtaining him directly from their stable mistress. Somewhat fewer resistant children but a higher ratio of females, all with blonde hair, I might add. He responds best with the use of the crop and pain. Especially waxing. He loves wax, don't you Twenty? As you can see, his former mistresses enjoyed using ball extenders on him.

"This exotic example of male pulchritude is JM62AA05BBFF. As you can see, he arrived from Japan. Their numbering system is rather different from ours so we refer to him as Seven as he was our seventh acquisition this year. He produces very exotic girls with an interesting eye shape. As of the moment, he has produced no males, which has been somewhat of a pleasure. He always seems to be eager so we don't know if he reacts to any particular techniques. He is

Story 5 The Barn

particularly well trained and always waits for the command to insert.

"The final male is admittedly a bit of a wild card. Not everyone likes long red hair. However, as you can see he carries it well, especially when it is long as it is now. He is direct from the Danish court, a son of the present Queen, herself. He is especially good with oral. A little high-spirited for my tastes, but your woman did say you trained studs as a teen. And, of course, your mother is still quite famous in the right circles for her skills. We call him Twenty One."

Lady Margaret smiled at the stable mistress.

"Excellent. They look like they will provide brilliant rides. I am impressed. Now, what about the female surrogates? I notice you don't have them present."

"No, we find the males are impossible to control in the presence of Desire Virus infected females. We'd rather they didn't injure themselves trying to cover the mares without supervision. We have three young grooms who will assist you, today. They should be quite capable of ensuring control in the covering and preventing any unfortunate mistakes.

"We'll introduce the females after you have eaten and refreshed yourself. We have selected two mares for you. F64A2205 is a honey blonde. F-five's six sisters by the same sire and mare were all resistant. Unfortunately, she was not. Rather a shame as she was the prettiest of the brood. She has already borne two resistant girls.

"The other female is called C-Two. She is black haired and of Irish stock. A very sad story that. She was born resistant, in fact. Unfortunately, she was infected during a nipple piercing of all things. Stupid jeweler used the same equipment on a stable and then used it on a free woman. Then the fool compounded her negligence with failing to properly clean her tools. As you know, direct injection of the virus almost always results in infection regardless of the resistance level of the injected woman. The jury sent the negligent bitch of a jeweler to Newgate for life as punishment, but the damage had been done by that point. We've kept poor C-Two here ever since. She seems to be a favorite of the males. This will be her first breeding. However, we have great hopes for her."

Story 5 The Barn

"Your reputation as a superior breeding facility does seem to be justified based on what you have said. However, the proof is in the tasting as my dear mother would have said."

"Thank you. We will endeavor to prove your trust justified. In the meantime, you must be hungry after your long ride. We have a meal prepared and waiting. Since you wish to participate, I would suggest you eat before we introduce the breeders. Unless, of course, you wish to take a bath first. In that case, we'll serve after your ablutions."

"Thank you. I am a touch peckish. We can begin the covering proper after my meal. I believe, I shall try the oral one during the meal. Twenty-one, I believe you called him."

The stable mistress bowed to Duchess Margaret and led her to the sitting room. Margaret gazed around the room at the thick rugs and ornate plaster fireplace. She nodded her head once and walked to a walnut and red velvet pleasure chair. Pulling it into the middle of the room, she climbed up into it, spreading her legs on the widely separated supports. She shivered as a cold breeze slid over her bare pussy where it hung between the well-padded supports. Within moments, two young women, barely out of their teens, entered. They were dressed identically in black leather riding breeches, and a black leather corset.

One of the women carried a black leather crop in one hand and guided the red-haired male by a short black-leather double lead she held in the other hand. The lead attached to the sides of a leather collar around his neck. The woman held the lead tightly, jerking it sharply downward from time to time. Each time she jerked the lead, the woman alternated blows on the male's ass with blows on his hard rod. Still the male rushed forward, eager to be put to his paces. Margaret smiled as she watched his antics.

The other woman pushed a dark walnut serving cart containing three silver cloche, and a tea service. Leaving the cart beside Margaret, she retrieved a half table on wheels from beside the fireplace. Wheeling the table to join the cart, the young woman selected a lace cloth, a white silk napkin, and silverware. The cloth floated onto the table and was soon joined by the napkin and the silver.

Story 5 The Barn

While the woman set the table, the other young woman guided the red-haired male to Margaret. Her crop flashed across the back of his calves and he dropped immediately to his knees. His hands lifted to hang by his throat, and he knelt panting between her outstretched legs. Alternating slashes of the crop on one ass cheek or the other with tugs on his leash, the woman maneuvered the male until he knelt with his mouth almost touching Margaret's cleft. His tongue hung over his lips and he whimpered. He gazed up at Margaret, longing bringing tears to his eyes. Margaret smiled and nodded at the groom. The woman's crop tapped the male's head just below where his braid began and he bent forward eagerly.

Margaret sighed and bent her head back as she felt his soft, wet tongue slide along her cleft. The tongue slid between the damp mounds of flesh, and flicked along the soft ridges of flesh that guarded her inner secrets. It slid from low on her cleft up to the hard nob that hid in a flap of skin at the top of her lips. Then back again, dragging soothing liquids over the lips. Sensation rolled around Margaret's groin, swelling her clit and driving a moan from her throat. She closed her eyes and rode the need until the first of many explosions rattled up her chest and burst in a gasp.

Margaret opened her eyes to see the table sliding over her lap. She felt a moment of regret at losing sight of the red-haired head bouncing between her legs. But the appearance of her meal soon reminded her that she hadn't eaten in several hours. Salad was first. Green and sweet, the lettuce was crisp and cool on her tongue. The dressing was cool and sweet, tasting of cucumbers and cream. It slid gently down her throat to mix with the delicate licking below that tickled her center. Margaret's tummy fluttered as the male's tongue slid over a particularly tender spot. She hummed in pleasure. Her eyes closed as she focused on the competing sensations.

Margaret's eyes burst open as the tongue slid between her inner lips and buried itself in the ridges of her tunnel. She slowly focused on the now empty silver platter of salad fleeing to be replaced by a steaming plate of red wine, beef and rice. Margaret breathed deeply, enjoying the musky sweet taste of Boeuf Bourguignon on her nose. Heavy hints of umami mixed with the fruity scent of the wine filled her sinuses. Her mouth watered and Margaret gulped as the tongue flicked against her clit. Her eyes widened as the tongue smashed repeatedly against the hard nob of flesh. Margaret cut into a darkened orange carrot and sucked on the taste of wine and beef as the mouth slid over her bud and began to softly suck at the rigid nob.

Story 5 The Barn

Margaret whimpered around a bite of beef and onion as the mouth slid along her slit. The tongue played over the soft folds, driving bursts of desire deep into her body. She could feel the swelling there, as the need built, liquid fire burning between her legs. Margaret chewed slowly, loving the taste and feel as the thick gravy squeezed from the dark brown beef. It mixed with the sweet onion at the back of her throat and slid down to mix with the swelling that fluttered over her mound. It slid from between her legs in a wash of liquid that dribbled over the male's chest, and then trickled down to drip liquid fire on his rigid cock. The tongue smashed harder against Margaret's pussy, milking the juices from her body, leaving her wet and slippery. Her inner tissues slid against each other dragging at the tongue that sucked along her lips. Margaret whimpered as the desire built and exploded between her legs. The red-haired male made soft bleating cries between her thighs.

All too soon, beef, carrots, onions, rice, and gravy had all been spooned into Margaret's mouth. They melted down her throat, leaving her sighing at the richness of taste and sensation. Her mouth filled with the sensations of tongue on pussy lips and clit. Margaret ran a hand down her stomach and over her hip. She caressed the male's head, pushing him deeper into the demanding cleft between her thighs. She moaned and gulped as his tongue pounded a tattoo against her clit. She seized his braid and pulled his head deeper into her, demanding his tongue, forcing his mouth against her.

Margaret's hands were shaking as she spooned heavy bread pudding and rum sauce from the silver bowl. The mix of sweet and pungent, lemon and rum, bread and sugar, whirled around her tongue filling her mouth with sweet liquid. The mix of tongue on lips, tongue on clit, and tongue sliding between her lips to play deep within her, whirled around her mound, filling her pussy with slippery liquid heat. Margaret cried out, a soft quick scream as the male's tongue found a particularly sensitive spot between her lips. His wet appendage slipped between the lips, playing with the soft tissues, twisting the loose skin, dragging sensations loose to build into a swelling of pressure somewhere below her heaving mound.

Margaret screamed as his tongue found her clit. It flickered over the hardness. It twirled around the hood, dragging the hard little bud into the open. It traced the hard bundle that ran from her clit to her brain. Margaret bounced her hips, pushing his tongue against her with every flex of her ass. His head bounced against her, fucking her with his mouth. Fucking her

Story 5 The Barn

with his chin, pushing the pressure out from her swollen cunt into her clit and bursting it in an explosion of light and fire from between her legs. Sweet syrup drained over her tongue and fled down her throat.

Her spoon tumbled from nerveless fingers. It struck the silver bowl with a high pitched belling and bounced. The handle hit the edge of the table and the spoon flipped end over end and twirled downward to bounce against Margaret's leg and then to skid across the floor. It rang with a high pitched belling as it struck wood, and metal, and stone.

Margaret moaned and screamed as the balloon between her legs burst raining desire down the male's chest. She overflowed, sensations chasing juices. It exploded within her groin, rippling up her spine until it burst from her throat in a scream of pure lust fulfilled. Margaret shook in the chair, her legs bouncing against the supporting legs. Her ass lifted and fell as it sought and then ran from the glorious tongue and it's painful overload of sensation. Her tits bounced on her chest, wobbling in their pleasure. Her nipples danced, hard buds that drew the eyes and twitched beneath the assault of sensation from her clit.

Margaret seized the male's head and forced his face deep within her slit, his nose buried between the swollen lips. His braid bounced, a soft woven cock growing from the red bush that grew above her clit. And still his tongue attacked her need, the soft wetness scraping along her hard bud and twisting around the delicate sensitive tissues that guarded her secrets. Her body leaked, juices dribbling down his chin and dripping on his chest. Her body spasmed, jerking in her need and the release that rippled through her.

Margaret pushed the table. It twisted and collapsed, bouncing on the stone floor with a high pitched crash that barely registered in her ears. The noise rattled, hidden by the thunder of blood pounding against her skull. Her chest heaved and her head thrashed from side to side. Her thighs crushed the male's head, squeezing every possible touch of sensation out of him and down the hard rigid shaft of her clit. It burned deep into her, exploding up her spine in a flare of pain and pleasure.

Margaret screamed once and then collapsed. Her chest heaved and her limbs shook. Her breasts bobbled in their leather cage. Margaret whimpered as the male continued to lick her rippling flesh.

Story 5 The Barn

Two of the grooms reached out, seizing the leash that hung down his back. They pulled hard, dragging the reluctant creature from his meal. The male fought, straining against the tightness. His face turned from pink to red to purple as he fought to return to his honey spring. The women pulled with both hands, pushing against the floor with both legs. Trapezius and Latissimus strained and outlined on their backs as they pulled against the reluctant votary.

One woman stumbled, losing her balance as the male finally collapsed to lay sobbing on the floor at Margaret's feet. The other groom lurched and her hand slapped against the cold stone as she too almost fell to her knees. Anger flashed over her brow, and she stared through tight eyes. Her arm flashed and the crop cracked against the male's skin. His flesh bounced and reddened but he lay sobbing against the cold hardness of the stone.

Margaret lay boneless in her chair. She cracked one eye and stared at the groom as the woman swung her crop against the back and ass of the heaving mound of the red haired male. Margaret sighed and smiled. She closed her eyes and breathed deeply. A light grating snore drifted from the chair.

Notes From the Author

A note from the author

I hope you enjoyed this book. I enjoy reading your mail so write me with any comments or things you'd like to see in coming books. You can send me mail at **jean.ecrivain@gmail.com**. You can also follow me in any of four different ways. On Facebook at http://www.facebook.com/jean.ecrivain. Or you can find me on Amazon at amazon.com/author/jeanecrivain. You can also find me on Goodreads and I maintain a website at https://jeanecrivain.wordpress.com/.

On Facebook you can follow my books, learn more about the characters, discover what my next book is about, when it is due, and generally shoot the breeze with me. You can also follow my individual series pages on Facebook.

On my website, you can signup for my newsletter, get free books, and find out about my promotions.

I'd love to hear from you. I won't promise to include your ideas, however, I do promise to read each and every one of your emails and comments. And I promise to at least think about your ideas. And of course, compliments are always appreciated. They might even make it into print!

And speaking of comments and compliments, one of the best things you can do to show your appreciation for this or any other book, is to write a review on Amazon or wherever you bought this book. Websites like Goodreads are other places to record your opinions. By doing so, you'll help other readers to make an informed decision.

To submit a review of this book on Amazon go to https://www.amazon.com/dp/1976423872 and select the review button.

About the Author

Jean Ecrivain lives on a private lake somewhere in Canada with her two cats, one dog, a library, a selection of adult toys, and her one 'special toy'. In early grade school, she discovered a love of reading when she fell asleep in class, pulled off the highest marks, and was rewarded with a book. The next year, she wrote a thirty page story about a horse and a girl in composition class and she has been writing ever since. Some time in her early teens she discovered boys and her writing took a decidedly different track.

She has worked many jobs from waitress to stripper, gas jockey to receptionist for an escort service. Today, she can be found either sitting at her computer thinking up new ways to express her fantasies or on the beach, in the woods, in the living room and sometimes, even in the bedroom living out those fantasies with her own 'special toy'.

Other Books by Jean Ecrivain

On Kindle:

A Taste for the Night Series
A Taste for the Night Book 1 Arrival
A Taste for the Night Book 2 Settling In

Chasing Fae Romance Series
Book 1 Well Met in Forest Light
Book 2 Well Met in Castle Light
Book 3 Well Met in Dragon Light (coming Nov/2017)

Steamy Shorts
Steamy Shorts 1
Steamy Shorts 2
Steamy Shorts 3
Steamy Shorts 4
Steamy Shorts 5

In Print:

A Taste for the Night Series
A Taste for the Night Book 2 Settling In
(includes Bonus of Book 1)

Chasing Fae Romance Series
Book 1 Well Met in Forest Light
Book 2 Well Met in Castle Light
Book 3 Well Met in Dragon Light (coming Nov/2017)

Steamy Shorts
Steamy Shorts 1
Steamy Shorts 2
Steamy Shorts 3
Steamy Shorts 4
Steamy Shorts 5

Samples

The Barn

Did you enjoy this book? Then you might enjoy The Barn.

Follow the adventures of Lady Margaret in the novella-length novel

The Barn

available FREE only on the author's website

"Your Grace. We find that the breeding takes best when the females are able to cum. I'm told that it is just a folk tale, but it is one we follow. Accordingly, we prefer to prepare the females well before a male is put to them. Since this is C-2's first time in the breeding pens, we prefer that she watch F-5 entertaining the studs first. That will, hopefully, remove her fear and allow her to cum when covered herself. It does mean that the breeding will take much longer but in return, your attention won't need to bounce from one mare to the other. Would you care to choose a method of preparation, Your Grace? We recommend the vibrators in this case. Although F-5 does occasionally enjoy light pain, we'd rather you didn't frighten C-2."

The stable mistress pointed to the black wood table containing the toys that Margaret had remarked on earlier. Margaret dipped her head and then glided over to the table. She spent several minutes perusing the selection of items. At one end of the table were the items exclusive to the male studs, ball stretchers, cock crushers, and so forth. At the other end of the table were the female items, dildos, clit jewelry, ben wa balls, and such. In the middle were the items for both, whips, nipple jewelry, cuffs, and so on. Margaret slowly perused the options, fingering some, picking up others. She picked up a heavy nipple weight and caressed its silver teardrop shape lovingly. However, looking at C-2 she frowned and put it back. Instead she selected four medium nipple weights, two clit weights, two dildo-shaped vibrators, and two anal vibrators with long horse tails. The dildo vibrators were not precisely dildo shaped. One consisted of a long curved shaft with a bulb at the end. Another thinner shaft grew from the handle. It ended in two thin probes. The second dildo was the perfect reproduction of an erect cock down to the veins that lined the shaft. It too had a longer thinner shaft growing from the black handle. This shaft, however, ended in a small brush-like affair. Handing her choices to the auburn-haired groom, Margaret sauntered back to the stable mistress.

"I believe these will suit admirably without frightening poor C-2. I assume you didn't intend to let the males use their arses under the circumstances. The horse tails should keep the mares excited between coverings", whispered Margaret.

"No, Your Grace, we allow limited use of their mouths but we'd rather not waste precious fluids. The poor dear studs are only able to produce so much. That's why we have twice as many studs as mares. I believe your choices are perfect for the mares. Since C-2 is not going to be in use immediately, I'm going to use Twenty-one to help her get ready. Shall we begin?"

The stable mistress poured Margaret a crystal goblet of Pommery while the auburn and black haired grooms approached the black haired C-2. Each of the grooms seized a breast and with a smile for each other bent and began to lick at the erect nipple. C-2's head snapped back and she moaned. Her hips began to flex in their bindings, circling and pumping as her excitement rose. The grooms' hands flexed and breast flesh compressed, forcing the hard buds out further. The wet tongues took full advantage, lapping at the hard nobs and flicking around the crinkling pink flesh that surrounded them. White teeth flashed and wet, red tongues pushed tender flesh against cutting edges. Tears slid over C-2's lids and trickled down her cheeks, dancing to her whimpers.

Fingers slipped over soft flesh, played and pulled on indentations. A concert played in duo for so long that fingers naturally followed fingers. Two hands acting as if they had a single body between. The fingers slid lower, tickling along swelling tummy, pulling and plumping, then tickling lower, playing on C-2's heaving mound. They trailed over lips and back along the cleft with the coordination born of long practice. Whimpers turned to moans and hips danced and quivered. Red lips pulled on hard nipples, drawing them out and teasing them until they stood well proud of white soft mounds.

The two grooms moved as one to clip the nipple weights on engorged nipples. C-2 let out a tiny shriek as she felt the crushing discomfort of a clip on her sensitive buds. She panted and her head hung down, spilling her dark hair between her round white breasts. Black and silver droplets hung from the purple tips, framing the black hair and white skin.

Fingers returned to a now well-soaked cleft. The two grooms played in the moistness for a moment, their fingers twisting and stroking C-2's sensitive flesh. They avoided her hard bud, focusing instead on the inner lips and the now leaking vaginal channel. As C-2's dancing grew wilder and her moans louder, the two grooms kissed her bent thighs, and slowly licked rippling skin from knee to crotch. Fingers moved upwards to the now hard bud in its mantle of sensitive skin. Fingers clasped the hard shaft between them, crossed and sharing the bud, palm to palm, lovers clasping hands over a well-loved flower. They stroked, softly, slowly, teasingly, up and down, slowly rotating over the sensitive head, while C-2's moans grew louder. Frustration turned to tears and moans to sobbing as relief was denied. Fingers prodded at the hood, pushing it back and revealing the moist man within. A squeezing of the clip and a light click brought a scream as C-2's head jerked up. The black and silver danced and tinkled between her upturned legs.

The grooms kissed as they stood, lips locked as bodies moved upwards as one. Their fingers trailed along C-2's thighs, twirling in the moistness. The grooms slowly moved apart, their eyes locked as they separated. They smiled softly. A blush rose over one woman's cheek, turning her skin red against the blackness of her hair. Deep breaths and four breasts heaved, shaking the red tipped nipples as bare breasts jiggled.

***

Want more of Lady Margaret's adventures?

The Barn

is available for **FREE** to subscribers of Jean's newsletter.

Sign up at

https://jeanecrivain.wordpress.com/newsletter/
***

 A Taste for the Night Book 1 Arrival

Did you enjoy this book? Then you might enjoy the A Taste for the Night series.

Follow the continuing adventures of Chantelle, Serena, and Lord Carnarvon in the full-length novel

A Taste for the Night Book 1 Arrival
and
A Taste for the Night Book 2 Settling In

available now on Kindle and Paperback

Serena took Chantelle by the hand and led her from the lobby into a nearby room. Chantelle could see antique Turkish carpets and even to her untrained eye they looked real, and very expensive. So expensive that Chantelle's heart skipped a beat as she was led onto them. Off to the side, Chantelle could sense overstuffed wing chairs and a couch of some sort. All she could see were the legs, but that was enough to understand the wealth to be found in this sitting room. Serena guided her to stand between the fireplace and a chair upholstered in deep red velvet.

"To start with submissiveness is a spice. Too much of it and the broth is spoilt. Look up at me, girl." Serena said. Chantelle stared straight ahead as Serena put a finger under her chin and raised Chantelle's head slowly to a more normal position. Chantelle focused on her Mistress's body as her head was raised. She noted the flair of Serena's hips and the soft hang of the dress over Serena's crotch and down her thighs. Chantelle sucked air as she noticed the soft swell of Serena's tits and the bare flesh of her cleavage. Serena's hair was black and hung down in soft waves pointing at her nipples. Chantelle suddenly realized those nipples were hard points and Chantelle felt a growing softness and slipperiness between her own legs in response.

"Ah, much better. Let's start by talking about the future – your future. And the rules. We must have rules after all or what would we be but animals. Yes, the rules. For the next ten years, this will be your home. It will shelter you and guard you. It will feed you and in return, you will feed it. For the first five years, clothing is forbidden to you. If you are good, sometime during that period, you will be allowed some basic

A Sample from A Taste for the Night Book 1: Arrival

coverings whenever others are present. But mostly you will be nude. During that time, it will be my pleasure to train you. At the end of five years, another will come, I will leave, and you will take my place. So it has been for hundreds of years, and so it will be for hundreds more. For the first five years, you are the lowest of the low. Anyone can take you. Servants, guests, myself, or the Master. You will obey them all. But only the Master is to receive your full submission and then only as he wishes it. You need not bow, or kneel, or avoid their eyes. Much of what you have been taught has not been followed for over a hundred years. I shall teach you what is now expected of you. I am second only to the Master and all obey my commands in this house save our Master, Lord Carnarvon. In time, they will obey yours, but for the moment, you are their toy. Do you understand?"

"Yes, Mistress, I understand." whispered Chantelle throatily.

"Good, then let us begin by dressing you properly. We have only a few hours until Lord Carnarvon awakes. You must be ready by then. The Master will be hungry and he loves his first taste of new flesh. Take off your clothes and place them on the chair beside you. Slowly now. Nudity is exciting only when it is savored. "

The squeak of the chair as a weight settled seemed to flow over Chantelle's spine. Slowly she began to undo the fastenings where the leather lace met the red choker. She remembered her training and she would do justice to this act of release. Chantelle's breasts began to heave as she felt the desire begin to flow between her legs. It was exciting to strip before this beautiful, powerful woman. In moments, the straps of leather began to peel away from her shoulders. Chantelle could feel the sudden chill as the straps fell away from her back. In the front, Chantelle carefully held the straps against her collarbone, keeping the illusion that the leather and satin still covered her breasts. When both straps had been undone and fallen away, Chantelle began to slowly lower her hands rubbing the soft black leather across the tops of her breasts. Her nipples sprang to attention, becoming hard nobs, as they were slowly uncovered. The touch of the satin backing on her nipples almost made Chantelle cry out but she held her voice just as she had been taught. Miss Stevens would have been proud; the only sound that escaped Chantelle's lips was a quick gasp. Chantelle weighed her breasts in her hand and flicked her thumbs over the tight, hard, little nipples. Each flick

A Sample from A Taste for the Night Book 1: Arrival

caused a clenching of her lower mouth and a tautness that ran from her clit up to her stomach muscles.

Chantelle's breathing caught in her throat and she dropped her breasts to grab the ends of the leather ribbons that secured her red corset. The sudden pain as her breasts bounced sent a ribbon of heat from her nipples to her clit. Chantelle's legs began to shake and she had to force her knees straight. She had practiced this many times before but the sexual tension now was much different from the practices. Chantelle could feel Serena's need and that need almost pushed her into a small orgasm.

The sudden release of pressure as Chantelle loosened the corset caused her to suck in a deep breath. Chantelle shook her blond locks in surprise. She hadn't realized that the corset had restricted her breathing that much. It seemed like the sudden influx of oxygen drove a stream of liquid from her insides. She could feel a flushing as her body loosed a stream of liquid lust from her lower lips.

Folding the corset became a meditation ritual. Chantelle took the opportunity of the break to calm her frayed nerves. If she didn't control her lust, she would come long before she could give the same pleasure to her Mistress. And that would never do. Chantelle could feel the shift as her breasts swung from bending over to place the corset in the chair. She almost cried out but instead bit her lip and slowed her breathing.

Turning back to Serena, Chantelle noticed that the white silk shift was still around her waist. The dress flowed over the cord that circled her waist and then hung down between her legs, its knotted ends banging slowly against her crotch. Chantelle began to caress her stomach, slowly massaging feeling back into the skin compressed by the corset. She ran her thumbs up and under her ribs. Her fingers flowed over the bulge of her tummy and down to the knotted cord. With a quick yank, the cord came loose and her dress flowed down her legs, to puddle about her feet.

Chantelle ran her hands down along her hipbones and across her thighs. She longed to run her hands over her lips and into the moist channel between them. But for the moment, she avoided touching the oh-so-soft skin at the junction of her legs. It was hard. The seeping moistness seemed to draw her attention and her hands. Her cunt burned and yet the outer lips were cold in the cool breathing of the house. Chantelle

A Sample from A Taste for the Night Book 1: Arrival

bit her lip and whimpered as she ran her hands over her inner thighs and up the sides of her groin. With a shudder, she stepped unsteadily out from the puddle of silk then bent down to retrieve the material from the floor. It took all of her control to focus on folding the silk into some sort of order and then place it on the chair beside herself. With a shudder and a small cry, she sank to the floor to crouch on her knees, her soft ass resting on her heels. Chantelle's head fell forward on her chest.

The scrape of the chair as Serena rose unsteadily grated on Chantelle's nerves. Chantelle could feel Serena leaning over her. She could hear Serena's uneven breathing. She could smell the heat rising from Serena. Serena's lust was a thin film coating Chantelle's tongue and burning her mouth.

"Oh, you are going to be so much fun. I could just eat you up. In fact, I think I will."

***
Follow the continuing adventures of
Chantelle in
A Taste for the Night Book 1 Arrival
and
*A Taste for the Night Book 2 Settling In
available now on Kindle and Paperback*
***

A Taste for the Night Book 2
Settling In

Did you enjoy this book?

Follow the continuing adventures of Chantelle, Serena, and Lord Carnarvon in the full-length novel

A Taste for the Night Book 1 Arrival
and
A Taste for the Night Book 2 Settling In

available now on Kindle and Paperback

Serena blinked. There was some sort of buzzing pushing through the fog in her brain. She yawned and stretched, feeling the warm arm of Chantelle clutching possessively at one breast. She grabbed the hand and pushed backwards into the warm softness at her back. She could feel twin pillows pushing into the skin either side of her spine. Serena smiled and cuddled closer.

But the buzzing continued, slowly gaining in volume. Serena sat up quickly finally realizing the source of the sound was the intercom on the opposite wall. She bounced out of bed and fairly flew to the door. The screens were first. Everything looked good. Only one man stood at the door, no one else in the hall. Serena put her eye to the small brass tube. Yes, it was the Master. She had practiced this ritual over and over. There were no mistakes. The switch on the intercom came next.

"Got it, my Master. Thank Heaven you're back. I'm working on the door now."

The lock was first. Heavy old-fashioned key in lock. Turn the key. Listen for the deep click of release. Remove the heavy metal lock. Put it on the shelf. Close the silk lined door on the shelf. Then hang the key below the intercom. Now check the screens again. Throw back the bolts and push on the heavy door.

Serena leapt at the figure standing in the doorway oblivious to his torn, bloody clothing. Lord Carnarvon stumbled backwards as the naked figure jumped to hang around his neck. His hands wrapped themselves around her and he buried his face in her

A Sample from A Taste for the Night Book 2: Settling In

hair. He could feel his neck grow wet from the tears of the softly sobbing bundle in his arms.

"I'm fine. We won. No one is hurt badly. We're fine. I told you we'd be fine," he mumbled into her hair.

Lord Carnarvon let Serena down when her soft form ceased to shake with her sobs. He held her at arm's length while he ran his eyes up her form, checking to make sure she was unharmed. Then he looked up guiltily to check on the nude form of Chantelle propped up on the bed. Chantelle quickly clambered out of the bed and dropped to her knees. Her head pointed downwards, eyes properly averted, hands on her thighs framing the delights between. Her soft breasts heaved, her tightening nipples drawing Lord Carnarvon's eyes.

Serena stepped back and for the first time looked at her Master. She saw his shirt, bloody and grass-stained, hanging in rags from his well-muscled chest. She saw the fresh blood smeared across his chest, and the trails of raw, red flesh where a claw had raked its way over his pectorals. She saw the bloody bite marks on his calf. Her eyes grew wide and her jaw dropped.

"Chantelle ... quickly! There's soap and cloths above the sink. Bring two of them. And a first-aid chest in the cupboard beside them. Hurry! Not hurt badly? Fuck, and damn. You look pretty bad to me. How are Thomas and Geordie? And Mrs. Cadmar?"

Serena leapt at Lord Carnarvon once again. This time she grabbed the remnants of his shirt and tore them away from him. Shaking with fear, her hands fumbled with the fastenings of his pants. It seemed to take forever, but soon Lord Carnarvon stood nude, his pants puddled around his feet, his skin covered in blood, grass, and the unidentified. Blood gleamed from several raw, painful looking wounds.

Chantelle gasped and stared at her master. Her eyes swept down his form from his eyes to his ankles, only to bounce back to stare at his groin. His soft penis curled over the hairless balls. Even his shaved groin had a raking cut on it. As she stared at the snake between his legs, it began to rise, growing harder and longer. Chantelle licked her lips and felt a moistness seeping between her legs.

A Sample from A Taste for the Night Book 2: Settling In

"Give me one of the cloths. You take the left and I'll take the right. We need to get this blood off him so we can clean the wounds. Stop staring girl. You can suck on him later. After we've sterilized the broken skin."

Serena's voice was shrill and frightened but it was enough to break Chantelle out of her dazed staring. Chantelle tossed a wet cloth to Serena and rushed to Lord Carnarvon's side. Beginning at his shoulders, she began to rub the blood and stains from Lord Carnarvon's skin. Brown rivulets ran over his chest and down his legs to puddle around his feet. It took several trips to the small sink before they finished.

Serena tipped a bottle of disinfectant onto a large sterile pad and began to clean Lord Carnarvon's wounds. He gasped as the cold, stinging liquid hit the tender flesh. His nipples crinkled under the onslaught of sensations. The pain of the disinfectant on raw flesh and the pleasure of warm hands on sensitive flesh warred up and down his spine, mixing into a cacophony of sensations. Serena could feel his hunger grow as she worked. But for now the hunger would have to wait while she dealt with his body. Her own nipples began to crinkle and harden as his hunger had its inevitable effect on her body.

Chantelle rushed back and forth, bringing clean supplies and taking the soiled rags from Serena. Her hands shook and her soft breasts and firm ass jiggled as she rushed from man to sink to garbage and back. She couldn't understand it as the wetness between her legs grew. She knew she should focus on his care, not the steadily straightening of the sausage between his legs. She should be worried about his pain, not the way he would taste rolling on her tongue. But knowing she should concentrate on nursing and doing so were two entirely different things. She shook her head and tried unsuccessfully to direct her attention back to the important things and away from the vision of his cock pounding into her virgin cunt.

Finally, Serena was finished bandaging the worst of Lord Carnarvon's injuries. She tipped her head back and let out a deep breath she didn't know she was holding back. She motioned to Chantelle, and then dropped to her knees at Lord Carnarvon's feet. She began to lick at his hip, running her tongue along the ridge of his hipbone. The salty taste of his skin sucked at her insides and the smell of sweat, soap and alcohol crawled along her nasal passages filling her head and

A Sample from A Taste for the Night Book 2: Settling In

driving all other thoughts from her mind. She ran her nose along the soft skin of his groin, reveling in the scent and the satiny feel.

Serena could sense Chantelle joining her, matching her actions. The soft feel of tiny hands gripping and flicking her nipples drove a ripple through Serena's crotch and up her stomach. Serena sucked air as the overwhelming need grabbed and pulled on her cunt drawing it up through her spine to her chest. Serena flattened her tongue and laved a trail from Lord Carnarvon's balls up along his leg and over his groin. Meeting Chantelle in the center, they fought a battle of tongue against tongue over the territory each claimed. Their heads dipped lower, matching each other in the defense of their claims on his groin. Their tongues only ceased to prick and pluck at each other when Lord Carnarvon's prick broke through between them.

Serena's red lips surrounded Lord Carnarvon's hot, stiff shaft, meeting Chantelle's over the hard sausage. She sucked the shaft from the balls up to the bulb at the tip, her red lips matched by Chantelle's own. Her tongue caressed the soft skin under the hood, causing Lord Carnarvon to moan. The taste of male was stronger here and her cunt began to weep steadily, a running stream of need. She began to lick at the soft, purple head of Lord Carnarvon's cock, alternating with Chantelle. Under the bulb while Chantelle's tongue danced over the top, then over while Chantelle sucked on the lower, their tongues danced a jig across his swollen prick. Lord Carnarvon whistled through his teeth, his legs shaking with the sensation of two talented women loving his cock.

Chantelle sat back on her haunches and puffed air into her lungs. She could feel every bounce of her generous tits and her nipples grew into tight points with the stimulation. She could feel the liquid running from her fount and down her legs to puddle beneath her. With a cry of pure lust, she dove for Lord Carnarvon's balls. She sucked one of the firm eggs deep in her mouth. Her tongue played in the soft skin, twirling and gathering it up in ridges of pleasure. Chantelle felt Serena's lips bounce against her cheek as Serena swallowed Lord Carnarvon's shaft greedily. She sucked him deep into her gullet only stopping when Chantelle's jaw blocked the way forward. Chantelle could hear Serena as she gobbled and sucked at the hard shaft inserted down her throat. Chantelle could hear Serena softly gagging as the bulb at the end of his rigid member throbbed against her uvula. Chantelle could feel Serena's jaw working to drag every possible bit of his cock deep within herself. Chantelle hummed softly

A Sample from A Taste for the Night Book 2: Settling In

to herself, feeling Lord Carnarvon's ball bounce between her tongue and palate. Her eyes turned up into her forehead and her heart pounded in time to the pulsing of his cock.

Serena drew her head back, her lips tightly encircling the shaft that filled her mouth. She stopped with her mouth barely covered the purple bulb. She was rewarded with a drop of salty, sweetness at the tip of his burning cock, which her tongue greedily licked off. Her teeth gripped the bulb, scraping along its softness, as she drew her head still further back until only the very end remained. Suddenly she dived, her mouth grabbing the free ball beneath the shaft. For a moment Lord Carnarvon was driven mad with pleasure at the feel of both Serena and Chantelle sucking on the twin eggs. The feel of Serena's tongue as it licked his scrotum and then stretched out to lick along the perineum was maddening.

Chantelle grabbed the shaft above her as soon as she felt Serena quit caressing it with her mouth. Her hand slowly pumped up and down, milking the salty sweetness out of his hose. Her tongue fought with Serena's over the silky soft scrotum that she had been sucking on. But her need was too great. With a groan she attacked the shaft, swallowing it in a single gulp, forcing it down her throat until she felt it painfully bump against the walls, filling her with its hardness. Her throat hurt but it was a good hurt telling her that she belonged to this man. The pain told her that he owned her body, soul, and mind. That she was his and only his pleasure mattered. The feeling was so intense that she almost came, her cunt bubbling and spraying salty liquids down her legs. Her insides were churning with a need so strong that she began to feel ill from it. Every little breeze was torture to a body that demanded release. A body that demanded to cum.

But it wasn't her time yet. Her Master had to release his cum first spraying it deep within her. Tears ran from her eyes in frustration as her virgin cunt spasmed and rippled beneath her. Chantelle began to strip up and down, swallowing more of his cock on every bounce. Almost allowing his cock to pop from her red lips before bouncing once again along the mighty tube. Her tongue played up and down the shaft. It traced the outlines of each of the bulging veins along his cock. Her tongue loving the taste of his saltiness and the softness of his hardness. Faster and faster she drove her head up and down his manhood, chasing the flood she knew was hers.

A Sample from A Taste for the Night Book 2: Settling In

Serena buried her nose in the soft bags of treasure between Lord Carnarvon's legs. Her tongue ran over his scrotum where it met the skin between his legs and up along the so sensitive crease. She could feel his clenching as he fought to delay the inevitable release. She chuckled to herself. She knew him too well. Chantelle could take his blessing this time, but it would be Serena's tongue that drove the salty jism to boil up from his balls and spray down her throat. It would be Serena that took away his control. Her tongue began to travel leaving a wet trail behind. Along the ridge between his legs first. And then beneath the balls. Around the crease and then across that so sensitive area where his cock and balls met. Serena could feel Lord Carnarvon's ass clench and his cock bounce with the intensity of sensation. Soon. So soon. He couldn't hold back much longer, she knew. Serena began to lave around his balls and across the oh-so-sensitive skin at the base of his cock. She could feel Chantelle's jaw bounce off her cheek with every downthrust.

Serena grabbed Chantelle's nipple between her thumb and forefinger and pulled hard. She twisted the hard nob and squeezed it while extending the breast as far as she could. Her timing couldn't have been better. No sooner had she clamped on Chantelle's tender nipple than Lord Carnarvon grabbed Chantelle's head and forced his cock deep into her throat. His shaft began to pump. Hot and thick his salty-sweet cum flew down Chantelle's throat. The first spray seemed to fly straight down to her stomach not touching the sides of her gullet. The second seemed to fill her gullet and the third filled Chantelle's mouth and began to overflow over her red lips and down her chin.

It was all Chantelle needed. She bubbled and screamed as her cunt clenched, expelling a stream of cum over her legs and the floor. She choked and gulped, expelling Lord Carnavon's cum out in a burst through her nose. Her body rippled and her eyes rolled up into her head with the intensity of her reaction. She grabbed the soft pillow of Serena's breast and Lord Carnarvon's leg to keep her balance. That was all that Serena needed. A bolt of pure pleasure burned from her breast to her cunt. Her own gash began to pulse sending shockwaves rippling up her body. A moan escaped her lips as the pulsing between her lips sprayed a fine mist of woman cum over the wall behind her. Serena collapsed, her muscles turned to jelly. Chantelle followed soon after, her head pillowed on the soft hip of the body below her, her body continuing to heave while ripples coursed through her from ass to shoulder.

***

A Sample from A Taste for the Night Book 2: Settling In

Follow the continuing adventures of Chantelle in
A Taste for the Night Book 1 Arrival
and
***A Taste for the Night - Book 2 Settling In
available now on Kindle and Paperback***

***

Chasing Fae Romance Book 1 Well Met in Forest Light

Did you enjoy this book? Then you might enjoy the first book in the Chasing Fae Romance series Book 1 Well Met by Forest Light by Jean Ecrivain.

Follow the continuing adventures of Sarah, and Robin (and Tara) in the full-length novel

Well Met by Forest Light

Available now in Amazon Kindle and Paperback editions

Sarah smoothed her black silk dress with red trim over her hips. The designer dress was exquisite, cut to emphasize, and fit like a glove. What there was of the material was thin enough to show Sarah's every curve and yet was thick enough to hide the black thong and stockings that had accompanied the package. Delicate gold chains crisscrossed the dress at a few key points, holding the material together, drawing the eye, and emphasizing the fit and the bare skin beneath. Sarah could feel the smooth silk rubbing over her nipples and the chill of bare skin between, teasing the sensitive flesh with every movement. A diamond and onyx necklace set off her blonde hair against the blackness of the dress and the deep décolletage, finishing the drop-dead look. A shiver ran up her bare back.

Tara whistled at Sarah. "Wow, these dresses are amazing. And you look hot, girl. Hotness number one sure has some taste. And money."

Sarah felt her pussy flutter as she checked out Tara. Her dress was the opposite twin to Sarah's dress. Red with black trim, it framed Tara's figure like a glove, displaying her breasts to perfection, and hiding the red thong and stockings that were her only undergarments. It covered only what was necessary and hinted rather openly at what was hidden. Delicate gold chains kept the swaths of material together. An onyx and diamond pendant, opposite twin to Sarah's own, completed the look. If Sarah's own reaction was any indication, any men they met tonight were going to be cleaning the floor with their tongues. And with a bit of luck later, the best would be using those tongues elsewhere.

Sarah shuddered with undisguised lust. She could feel her pussy lips growing slick and her tummy

A Sample from Chasing Fae Romance Book 1: Well Met in Forest Light

flipping with the growing desire. Sarah shook her head to clear her thoughts of Tara, tongues, and strong male shoulders and thighs. What was wrong with her? Today had been an unending sequence of orgasms and still she wanted more. And from Tara's labored breathing and shiny eyes, Tara was ready to experience another set as well.

Sarah and Tara both jumped at the noise of the black stretch limousine pulling up to the shop. They both blushed and exchanged a guilty glance. As one, they sucked in air, forcing their breasts out, displaying their hard nipples against the silk of their dresses.

With just a minimum of fuss, they handed the flower arrangement over to the formally uniformed driver. He placed the display in the vehicle and then returned to open the door for them with a deep bow. Sarah and Tara both smiled as the silent uniformed driver opened the door to the car and helped them into the empty vehicle.

Sarah and Tara sank into the soft black leather as the vehicle floated off into the traffic. They giggled and exchanged a glance as they noticed two small packages sitting on the bar top addressed to them. With a small amount of confusion as they identified which was their own, they opened the packages to find a pair of expensive jeweled bracelets. On the packages were two identical notes that read:

"Please accept and wear this gift of apology. I had wished to collect you myself. However, I find that I am unavoidably delayed. An unacceptable lapse on my part, for which I beg your indulgence. The driver will collect you and then myself, a trip of perhaps one half hour. We can then proceed to the party. In the meantime, there is champagne in the bar. Please feel free to indulge.

– N.D."

Sarah's eyes burned into Tara's chest as she bent forward to pour two glasses of champagne. Tara's tits swung freely giving Sarah a clear view of the taut nipples and the soft white swell of Tara's firm breasts. Tara handed Sarah one of the chilled crystal goblets and then trailed her finger languidly down the channel between Sarah's own firm melons. So focused were they on each other that neither noticed the windows of the limousine darken to opaque as they drove.

A Sample from Chasing Fae Romance Book 1: Well Met in Forest Light

* * *

Neo climbed from the limousine first ignoring the proffered hand of the silent driver. His black tuxedo seemed to billow around him as he swung around to offer his hand to assist Sarah as she climbed out behind him. Sarah watched as Tara followed behind, her breasts hanging down, displaying hard pink nipples crowning the soft cushions. She knew her own body had been on similar display. Sarah looked at Neo curiously. Although he certainly hadn't looked away, neither he nor the driver seemed to be reacting to either Sarah or Tara's enticing display. Sarah could feel her own lower body flutter at the display and her pussy lips grow slick. But the cut of both men's trousers remained perfect. Even their eyes did not seem to caress Tara's charms despite the brazen display.

Sarah shook her head. Her face lit up with a smile that only she could tell was false. Years of selling customers she couldn't care less about, products she couldn't stand held her in good stead. Only her eyes might have given her away had anyone chosen to look closely. A quick glance at Tara noticed a similar look of concern flit over her friend's face.

Sarah gaped up at the great Victorian home that greeted them. Perfectly manicured lawns led to a hedge of rose bushes in full bloom beneath a long porch. Great white columns stretched up two stories along the front porch, framing the massive oak doors. The massive steps leading up to the porch balanced the balcony running the width of the house. The clapboard siding was stained a dark, Lincoln green with white facings and gingerbread. A light orange glowed from the windows and the sound of a harp trickled over the dull roar of partygoers.

Sarah took a deep breath inhaling the scent of honeysuckle, roses, and pine. The sweet assault on her nose left her slightly lightheaded. The feel of her hard nipples slipping over the silk of her dress sent a flutter of desire rippling down her spine to pool between her legs. The cool evening breeze fluttered up her dress leaving a clenching in her groin.

Neo offered an elbow to each of the friends and proceeded to ascend the stairs with a lady on each arm. The driver followed behind, his arms filled with the massive flower arrangement. The door seemed to flow open without any signal from the party. As if the individual at the door had been waiting and watching just for them.

A Sample from Chasing Fae Romance Book 1: Well Met in Forest Light

A sea of bodies, and eveningwear in every hue greeted them as they entered the massive home. Low cut gowns framed and displayed firm breasts of every description. Tuxedos emphasized strong chests and shoulders. Strains of a small jazz ensemble wove through the low roar of the crowd. The high, sweet notes of the harp at the ensemble's core picked its way through the deep rumble of conversation and the occasional high giggle or deep laugh.

Sarah watched as a pretty, young girl flitted through the crowd. She couldn't have been much over 20 and was tiny and petite. Yet, she hefted a heavy tray filled with glass goblets above her head. Her short-cropped brown hair bounced as she bobbed and weaved amongst the guests. Her black and white maid's outfit flashed between the bright colors of the crowd. Other male and female servers similarly clad, flitted amongst the guests in other areas of the massive ballroom.

Neo scooped two crystal goblets of champagne from the girl's tray and handed them to Sarah and to Tara. With a hand on the skin of their lower backs, just above the jut of their round asses, Neo guided them further into the crowd. Behind them, forgotten, the silent driver disappeared with his burden.

***

Follow the continuing adventures of
Sarah, Robin, and Tara in
Chasing Fae Romance Book 1 - Well Met In Forest Light
and
Chasing Fae Romance Book 2 - Well Met in Castle Light
available now in Kindle and Paperback editions

and

Chasing Fae Romance Book 3 - Well Met in Dragon Light
coming soon in Kindle and Paperback editions

***

Chasing Fae Romance Book 2 Well Met in Castle Light

Did you enjoy this book? Then you might enjoy the first book in the Chasing Fae Romance series Book 2 Well Met by Castle Light by Jean Ecrivain.

Follow the continuing adventures of Sarah, and Robin (and Tara) in the full-length novel

Book 2 Well Met in Castle Light

Available now in Amazon Kindle and Paperback editions

Sarah shifted on her saddle as her horse stamped nervously on the cobblestones that lined the courtyard. She slipped her body forward and back unsuccessfully seeking a comfortable position. Her lips grimaced as she placed weight on her tender ass. She sucked air and moaned between clenched teeth as the saddle slipped between her lips over her clit.

"Why, in God's name, are we riding this morning? I'd much rather be lying in bed and doing other things than this", she whined.

"I understand thy desires, my love. But mine guests expect a Wild Hunt every morn and I must not disappoint them. And we must be present for at least one of the hunts."

"But chasing a poor little fox with horses and dogs? It's barbaric. It's hardly a fair fight. And I somehow think that it is rather unlikely that the poor creature is a pest whose population needs to be kept down. Not here, where a little magic could do the job much more effectively. You sure as hell don't need to raise a body this large to kill the poor thing. And I've yet to see a chicken in the whole country, so you can't be worried about them. About the only good thing that can be said about all this hoopla is that I get to wear a proper riding outfit and sit astride the saddle rather than that bloody sidesaddle stuff putting my leg to sleep. Even if this outfit does have rather more bare spots than I'm used to having in a riding habit."

"And a most fetching outfit it is, my love. The open shirt doth display thy bare breasts most fetchingly. The belt doth clench thy waist in a most titillating way. And the straps of thy riding trews art most cleverly placed to preserve thy modesty while leaving much bare to imagination and desire. Wouldst that I could explore the bareness afore we ride out. We shall have

A Sample from Chasing Fae Romance Book 2: Well Met in Castle Light

to find ourselves bereft of our guests before the day is done and my control is lost."

Sarah smiled to herself and shifted once again along the saddle. She could feel her pussy bleat and grow wet and slippery. A crawling sensation began between her legs and crept around her groin and ass. Her nipples formed sharp points against the linen shirt.

"But methinks thou dost mistake our prey for this day. There are no small animals in our lands; save those few we desire as guests. We would never kill them intentionally. And our borders are sealed from the young under-fae. Should one slip past our guards, they are hunted by the servants and slain. Our prey is much harder to hunt and much more enjoyable in the capture. Unless I am mistaken, they doth approach."

Sarah looked at where Robin indicated. Two young Kitsune females stumbled towards the company at the end of a long chain. They were so similar in looks that they could have been twins. Their hands were bound in front of their nude bodies by smaller chains attached to one large chain that split to end in black leather dog collars at their neck. Their identical red hair flowed between their elongated ears and down their back. Their breasts were firm and their nipples were hard, tight little buttons on white hills. Three black-tipped red furry tails swung from each round ass.

"Well, vixens, art thou both ready? Thou knowest the rules of the Wild Hunt. If thou canst avoid the huntsmen until the setting of the sun, each may choose a body slave from amongst the huntsmen for the duration of our time here. If thou art caught before the sun doth set, then thou wilt serve the huntsman or men and any hounds who art lucky enough to capture thee. Thou hast won a full half-hour of flight afore we follow. What say you?"

"We need only five minutes to leave your hunt behind. We will choose our mates regardless of the outcome. Shall I spend the remaining time with my hand between my legs? Your hounds will then have something to follow. I will still win this contest and the one to follow, my lord." The bolder of the two chimed.

"I think not, vixen. Methinks thou both doth leak enough already for e'en the most nose-dead hound or fae. Twenty minutes watching you pleasure yourselves would leave the hunt rutting the ground and

A Sample from Chasing Fae Romance Book 2: Well Met in Castle Light

unable to follow. So be off with you then. In five minutes we shall follow."

The bolder Kitsune smiled and waggled her hips. Her hands clasped the gold ring of her black leather chocker for a moment. They slipped to her breasts as the chains were removed and she flicked her thumbs over the hard nipples. One hand slowly drew down her body until she inserted a single finger between lips of her cunt. She rubbed it up and down her wet pussy and then withdrew its wet length. She ran the finger slowly up her body taking special care to circle her nipple. When she was sure she had everyone's attention, she stuck the finger between her lips and slowly sucked it dry with a smile. She stuck her tongue out and bowed to the company. With a laugh, she bounded out of the gate and dashed through the meadow beyond.

As soon as the chain was pulled from the silver buckle of her collar, the quieter Kitsune simply dropped both hands, spread her pussy lips, and flicked her fingertips over her lips and clit. Her hips bucked uncontrollably and her quick breathing set her heavy tits jiggling. She closed her eyes, sighed once, and whimpered. She threw a kiss to the crowd and then bounced out of the gate in quick pursuit of her sister.

Robin shook his head and chuckled. He looked at the astonishment on Sarah's face and his chuckles became a full-blown laugh.

"Not quite the prey thou expected, my lady love? Or the prize? All of our guests may choose to test themselves this way and enjoy the bounty. Though in truth, it is always the Kitsune that seem to be the first to volunteer. I think they are as excited by the hunt as they are by the reward. Today we hunt twin sisters. Tomorrow, we hunt a male. I understand most of the women have a bet amongst themselves as to which will find him first. Or whom he will chose to allow to capture him if one wishes to be more truthful. Our party, are not so caring. They, I am feared to say, are simply drunk on lust and longing."

"That was cruel. Making me think it was a fox we were hunting. I suppose you think you're a big man tricking me that way. Just you wait, mister comedian. You'll get yours."

A Sample from Chasing Fae Romance Book 2: Well Met in Castle Light

Robin sidled his horse up to Sarah, reached over, and kissed her deeply. His tongue slipped between her lips and claimed her mouth, flicking over the warm, moistness it found there. Sarah sighed and bent her head back sucking him deep into her mouth. Her tongue flicked along his, teasing him to enter her further.

"I already have mine and I am yours whenever thou wish it. And the sooner we can be lost from our company the happier I shall be."

"Typical man. It's only yours when I choose to give it to you ... but this is mine whenever I want," whispered Sarah sliding her hand between his legs.

Robin groaned and curled over her hand. His hand grabbed hers and held it against his hardness. Sarah smiled at the heat and the growing hardness beneath her palm.

"Now, it is thee who art being cruel, my lady. How shall I ride like this?"

Sarah smiled and squeezed his hard rod.

"Well you'll just have to find a way to soften it, won't you? You'll have to catch me first, though. Until then, you'll just have to ride behind me and settle for the view! Just like this!"

Sarah laughed. She slid her hand along his cock one last time, and put her heels to her horse. The tall, white beast leapt forward, and out the castle gate in close pursuit of the baying hounds and their erstwhile masters.

Robin pushed his hard cock into a more comfortable position, shifting his butt on the saddle. He guided his horse out the gate. As soon as he had cleared the gate and the few stragglers, he stood up in his stirrups, gave his horse its head, and raced across the meadow in pursuit of his prey.

* * *

Sarah stood up in her stirrups and clenched her ass. She longed to massage the soreness out but that would hardly be ladylike. She grinned to herself. Last

A Sample from Chasing Fae Romance Book 2: Well Met in Castle Light

night had hardly been ladylike either. Sarah closed her eyes, and licked her lips as she remembered sucking on both Robin and the faun's cocks. The evening had ended with one last fuck with one cock in her cunt and another in her mouth. Sarah hummed as her cunt clenched over the memories.

Sarah looked over at Robin and licked her lips. He had been behind her for most of the last six hours. And for most of the time it was quite obvious he had a raging hard-on. Sarah giggled. She had spent as much of her time finding a reason to lift her ass off the saddle and shake it as she had spent chasing the fox-women. She kept finding different ways for her tits to bounce out from behind her shirt only to be pushed back into hiding with a great flurry of attention-getting sound and motion. Robin now looked like he was ready to fall on his knees and beg her for relief. But Sarah hadn't quite finished teasing him yet.

Sarah giggled evilly to herself. She shifted her hips and enjoyed the slick feeling between her cunt lips. The crotch of her trews was wet and sticky, and the bare patches along her upper thighs glistened. The leather of her saddle was stained dark brown and her pussy was clenching and twisting every time she moved.

Just then, she noticed movement in a clump of grass on the other side of the meadow. With a quick laugh at Robin, she urged her horse into a canter and rode off after the waving signal. Robin shook his head, rubbed his crotch for the fifth time that hour, and rode quickly after her flashing white form.

As Sarah neared the waving clump of grass, she noticed a small red and white form running off through the turkey frond and bluegrass. With a quick shout at Robin, she urged her horse to a fast gallop and chased after the bounding Kitsune. But within moments, the only thing Sarah could see was the occasional wag of the tall grass to indicate where the Kitsune had run. Sarah chased the will-o-the-wisp for a few minutes but soon slowed to her mount to a walk. She swiveled her head around looking unsuccessfully for any sign of the prey. Within moments, she heard the noise of baying hounds.

Sarah stopped below an old, gnarled apple tree and watched as a faun and two hounds leapt on the shy Kitsune, bringing her down in a pile of laughing, naked

A Sample from Chasing Fae Romance Book 2: Well Met in Castle Light

forms. Sarah rubbed her pussy with one hand as she watched the sexy dog pile below her.

The Kitsune twisted around and slid down the faun's body. Around her, the hounds whined and licked at any body parts they could reach. Their cocks grew hard and were soon pointing towards the ground, dripping slickness on the ground below them. The Kitsune slipped back, the silver ring of her collar slid along the faun's hard cock sending shivers up his groin. The Kitsune grabbed the faun by his hard prick and pulled him towards her open mouth. She soon had herself twisted around with her ass and tails pushed high in the air and her hands and knees on the ground. Her cheeks began to puff out as she sucked the faun deep into her throat.

One hound pushed his muzzle deep into her pussy and began to lick with long strokes of his tongue. The other two hounds began to lick and nuzzle at her breasts. The Kitsune moaned and pushed her breasts at the two hounds. One of the hounds pulled back and shook himself. He rolled over on his back, his rock hard cock sticking straight up and his paws clawing at her body. His skin began to roil and bubble, the flesh molding and folding in on itself as he changed into the form of a dark-haired male. He howled and pulled himself under the Kitsune. His mouth plastered itself to her tit and he sucked the hard nob deep into his mouth. The Kitsune howled around the hard rod in her mouth and rolled her hips, pushing her cunt tighter against the hound that licked between her legs.

The Kitsune ground her hips against the hound, forcing his tongue to lash over her clit and lips. Her hips shifted from side to side as she sought to force his tongue against just the right spots. Wet slurping sounds drifted up as the hound licked and sucked on her flesh. He seized her lips between his teeth and sucked deeply on them. The Kitsune moaned. Her hips bucked and shook. Her feet pounded a drumbeat into the soft loam.

Her hands grasped the faun's thighs and forced him even tighter against her until she buried her nose in the soft fur above his hard rod. Her moan turned into a keening wail as she sucked the faun's cock deeper into her mouth. Her throat and cheeks worked as she sucked and licked along his length. She sucked at him as if she had been starved for days and he held the sweetest desserts. The faun seized her head and fought to keep his hips from bucking uncontrollably in response. His balls bounced off her chin drawing a whimper from him on every moist impact. He threw his

A Sample from Chasing Fae Romance Book 2: Well Met in Castle Light

head back and arched his back. A groan squeezed itself from between his lips.

The hound below her ground his penis into the soft loam. His jaws began to snap at her breast. His tongue flicked out, seeking out her hard nipple and drawing it between his sharp teeth. The hound seized on the nipple and drew it out as far as he could. He shook his head causing the heavy breast to bounce against the Kitsune's other breast and the other man-dog's cheek. With a growl, the hound swallowed more of the heavy flesh. His cheeks flared as his tongue flipped over the hard brown nob and the white flesh.

Beneath her, the man-dog twisted until his body was beneath the Kitsune. His hands and mouth continued to work the breast he had seized. He squeezed and rolled the flesh in his hands. White flesh squeezed out between his fingers and slowly turned pink. His tongue flicked out and over the hard, brown tube that crowned her breast. The Kitsune's moans rang off the trees that ringed the meadow. Tears ran down her cheeks.

The man-dog rubbed his hard cock along her slit. A long slick line of pre-cum formed along her mound and over her lips. The hound behind licked along her slick cunt and over the lips. It whimpered as it licked her mound clean. The Kitsune screamed as she felt the hard rod slide between her sopping wet lips and slide into the cavern between her legs. She slid down the hard cock and forced her crotch against the hot flesh below. Her ass rippled and heaved as she sought to draw more of the heat within her.

Behind her, the hound rooted in her ass, seeking the brown hole that hid between her soft cheeks. His long, hot tongue slid within the tight hole, forcing more whimpers from the Kitsune's lips. Her hips pounded on the man-dog beneath her, driving his hard rod deeper into her burning flesh. The hound rammed his tongue deep into her ass, keeping time with the rhythm of the wet slapping beneath him. His hips began to shake. Pre-cum rained off the hard cock between his legs in great drops. He whimpered and sucked his tongue out from between the soft pillows of her arse.

The hound pulled away, shook his head, and then clambered over the heaving form of the Kitsune. His hard cock stood out from his body, the tip red and glistening. He slid it between the soft cushions of the

A Sample from Chasing Fae Romance Book 2: Well Met in Castle Light

Kitsune's arse. He gripped her cheeks, separating them and giving him a clear view of the crinkled hole below her whipping tails. His cock curved slightly as it was trapped for just a moment. However, with a slight plop the head squeezed through the tight sphincter, stretching it and then sliding through. The hound threw its head back and howled. His paws slid around the Kitsune to grab and hold her waist between his legs. His hips heaved once, twice, slowly on the inward thrust and faster on the withdrawal as if pushing against a mighty spring. The strain of holding back set the hound's thighs to quivering, and soon the thrusts matched the jackhammering of the cock pounding into the Kitsune's cunt. The Kitsune quivered between the two cocks as they pounded into her cunt and ass, pulling out in lockstep and then pounding in to squeeze her sensitive flesh between their thrusting groins.

The Kitsune pulled her head back, sucking hard all the while and then thrust hard down the faun's cock. Her tongue slid down his hard pole and her teeth slid lightly along the soft skin drawing the prepuce back over the glans and teasing the hard flesh beneath. The faun began to hump her mouth, treating her throat like a soft, wet pussy.

The Kitsune grabbed the prick of the hound at her breast. Her hand slid over the soft, wet glans and then back down the hard shaft. She clutched at the hound's balls for just a moment, including them in the package she held. She drew them up with her hand until she reached the furthest extent she could stretch them. Then she slid her hand back down the shaft. The skin of his cock grew slick and hot. Over and over, her hand slid up and down the hard rod, up and down twice, then catching the balls and stretching them with her pumping hand as far as they would go, then back down again. Repeatedly her hand flew jerking on his prick twice then jerking balls and prick. The hound moaned against the breast, his screams vibrating against her hard nipples and shaking her aching tit.

With a howl, the hound rammed his cock against the Kitsune's hand. A long spray of white cum flew from the bright red end of his hard prick. It flew over her back in spurts to land in a long trail over her back and down the side of her breast. She shivered and shook as she felt the hot gelatinous mass strike her body.

She screamed against the body of the faun. The faun arched his body. He clenched her hair tightly in his fists as his spasming cock slipped from between

A Sample from Chasing Fae Romance Book 2: Well Met in Castle Light

her lips, spraying hot cum over her face. Long strands of liquid heat sprayed upwards into her hair to trail down over her eyes, her cheeks, and her chin.

Her hips bucked and shook as her own orgasm rippled up her backbone. Behind her, the hound ground his cock further into her ass. He panted and gasped as his hips shook with the force of his own orgasm. His tongue lolled out of his open jaws and his skin rippled and shifted until he collapsed and rolled off her. Long strands of cum stretched between his now softening prick and her ass. His skin twisted as his torso turned human, and then dog, and then back to human again.

Beneath her, the man-dog grunted and rammed his groin against the Kitsune's cunt. He rode her heaving hips, trying desperately not to slip out while her hips bounced and weaved in her orgasm. His hips were raised and his body arched into a pelvic tilt lifting her knees off the ground. White trails of liquid slipped over his balls and down his stomach. His head flew back dragging her tit until the nipple popped from his mouth. He held the position, his body shaking in time to her spasms, until with a groan he collapsed, dragging her unmoving form down to splay on ground in a pile of softly heaving bodies.

***

Follow the continuing adventures of
Sarah, Robin, and Tara in

Chasing Fae Romance Book 1 - Well Met In Forest Light
and
Chasing Fae Romance Book 2 - Well Met in Castle Light
available now in Kindle and Paperback editions
and
Chasing Fae Romance Book 3 - Well Met in Dragon Light
coming soon in Kindle and Paperback editions

***

Chasing Fae Romance Book 3
Well Met in Dragon Light

Did you enjoy this book? Then you might enjoy the final book in the Chasing Fae Romance series Book 3 Well Met by Dragon Light by Jean Ecrivain.

Follow the continuing adventures of Sarah, and Robin (and Tara) in the full-length novel

Book 3 Well Met in Dragon Light

Available soon in Amazon Kindle and Paperback editions

Moriko almost missed the small shop as she passed it. Moriko couldn't read the English writing on the wooden sign above the shop. But the mix of flowers and metal in the window bore the distinctive touch of Sarah. Moriko stared at the display, her hands grasping at the smooth glass, her nose crushed against the coolness.

Inside the shop, a young woman dressed in a red corset and black dress stared out at Moriko. Her hands were squeezed to her cheeks and a bouquet of orange gerbera lay at her feet. Moriko stared back then pushed herself off the window pane. The door squeeked and a bell rang. Moriko stopped as soon as she had crossed the threshold and bowed deeply, her hands sliding along her thighs as she bent.

"Honorable Lady Tara? I am Moriko, a friend of your friend Sarah and her paramour Robin of the Green. May I enter and speak with you about them. They are in great trouble and I am in sore need of your help."

Tara bobbed her head, her jaw flapping with the movement. Her eyes were wide and she stared at Moriko. Tara took a deep breath then patted her bare breast above her red leather sweetheart corset. She shook her head and squealed a short, high-pitched whine.

"You. You're a Kitsune. You're Fae. I can tell. I can see your disguise like a ghost around you, but I can see you clearly underneath. Oh, man this is so rad. I love your Japanese schoolgirl look. And those pointed ears are super hot. Oh, wait ... are you a cool Fae or a bad Fae? Is that why you can't cross my threshold. Is it like they say about Vampires, you need permission to cross a threshold? Look, if you're a cool Fae, I give you permission to enter ... as long as you bring no ill to me

A Sample from Chasing Fae Romance Book 3: Well Met in Dragon Light

... or any of my customers ... or my friends. Mustn't forget my friends."

Moriko blinked, shook her head and stared at the girl bouncing in excitement before her.

"Umm ... no, I'm just Fae. And I'm not cool. In fact, I'm rather hot at the moment. I've travelled far, and under difficult conditions to find you. And I'm tired, and I hurt, and I'm sweating, and frankly, I feel like something a farmer scrapes off his shoe. And your bouncing is making me ill. And as for good or bad, I'm just me. I try to be honorable but ... Could you please not bounce like that? And strictly speaking, I'm over your threshold already. Please don't bounce. I was just being polite as my honorable parents and governess taught me. Oh, and thank you for the compliments but I really need to discuss something with you. Can you please stop bouncing? Something that isn't for others' ears. Please, enough with the bouncing already. And I'm sorry if I caused you to drop your pretty flowers. Let me help you pick them up."

Tara looked down, seeing the mess of flowers at her feet for the first time. She gasped and dropped to her knees. For a few moments, she focused on picking up the orange gerbera one stem at a time. Her hands shook as she slowly circled, gathering the green and orange blossoms. Her breathing slowed as the simple act of carefully gathering flowers calmed her. She gasped as her hand clutched at the last stem and seized Moriko's hand instead. Tara slowly looked up to stare deep into Moriko's dark eyes.

Moriko stared deep into Tara's hazel eyes. She traced the colors as Tara's eyes shifted from green to brown and back again, while Tara stared deep into her own black pupils. Her eyes traced the soft heavily mascaraed lashes that lined Tara's eyes. Moriko's mouth opened and she sucked air over her lips in a whistle of almost desire. Her eyes slid down tracing Tara's nose and the slipping around the red lips. She focused on Tara's plumpness, as a wave of wanting forced her thoughts to dig deeply between the plump, red lips. Moriko's head tipped and her mouth opened in desire. She dived towards the target of her desire, tongue seeking, lips hunting.

Moriko and Tara met in a deep kiss that sent shocks of fire and heat through their mouths. Tongues met in a battle as old as time, sabre shocked against sabre. Breath flowed around and past their tongues

A Sample from Chasing Fae Romance Book 3: Well Met in Dragon Light

filling the other's mouth with the taste of desire. Moriko's hand sought out Tara's cheek as her tongue slipped around Tara's teeth, tasting the honey, seeking the soft wet flesh deep in the cavern of her mouth. Moriko hummed into Tara's mouth until both their ears rang with the deep vibration.

Moriko gently caressed Tara's cheek. Her finger sought out Tara's short black hair, and combed gently through the soft tresses. Her mouth crushed Tara's softness, sucking on Tara's lower lip, her tongue tickling the moist flesh. Moriko moaned as her tongue slid against Tara's teeth, slowly forcing its way between the ivory gates. Both women moaned as Moriko's tongue slipped within the hot, wet cavern of Tara's mouth. Tara's tongue flicked out and fled alternating pushing the invader out and drawing it within until both women were gasping in desire.

Slowly both women sat back on their haunches, reluctantly breaking their kiss. Moriko stared at Tara's eyes through a blurred curtain. Her breath came in gasps that bounced her bare breasts on her chest. It was matched by Tara's own gasps that threatened to dislodge her breasts from the low cut corset. Moriko's eyes fled to chase down Tara's shoulder until she stopped, fascinated by the soft round flesh cupped in leather.

"Ummm ... I wasn't quite ... Forgive this unworthy ..."

"Ummm ... Yeah, that was ... Maybe I better close the shop and lock the door."

The lock on the door made a solid clunk. It echoed through Moriko's stunned ears, and rattled for a moment through the fog that seemed to fill her chest. A second click and the room went dark. Only the light from the street illuminated the wooden counter that Moriko sat staring at. A red light blinked from the window, throwing fire over the hand that reached down so invitingly to the stunned Kitsune.

"I don't know if this is some kind of Fae magic thing, but I really hope that kiss was an offer or I'm going to feel really foolish in a moment. Uhm ... we can get some privacy in the back office if you'd like. I don't normally do this kind of ..."

A Sample from Chasing Fae Romance Book 3: Well Met in Dragon Light

Moriko silenced the babbling human with a kiss that quickly slid into an offer. Clutching each other tightly in an embrace that burned with desire, the two stumbled behind the counter and slid to their knees. Moriko's hands slid along the heavy leather corset, tickling at the glimpses of hot flesh beneath. They slid up the sides of the leather and along Tara's bare arms. Arms that had reached out to grasp Moriko's shoulders. Tara slipped one hand down the shoulder to grasp Moriko's soft breast. Tara's fingers molded the mound, pushing and prodding at the pliant flesh. A hard bud soon teased at Tara's palm and her finger flicked across the steadily hardening nob, drawing a gasp and a moan from deep in Moriko's stomach.

Moriko's hands slid beneath the hard leather. They tickled along Tara's waistband and then bounced over the leather ribbons that held the corset tight. Moriko's hands shook as she tugged and fought the ribbons, pulling frantically at the dangling strings. The bands released suddenly and the corset bounced apart, displaying more white flesh to Moriko's hungry eyes. Her eyes devoured the white flesh, relishing the blackness swallowing the whiteness, hard embracing soft, rigid against the pliant mounds. Moriko whimpered in her need.

Tara's nipple felt soft and silky on Moriko's tongue. The slight taste of salt merged with the sweet taste of her flesh leaving Moriko's tongue sparking with sensation. The tiny bud hardened in Moriko's mouth. It scraped along her palate leaving a trail of desire, a longing to suckle the soft flesh, drawing it deep into Moriko's mouth. Moriko's jaws worked, palpitating the soft mound, stretching the hard bud in the vacuum of her mouth. Tears flowed down Moriko's cheeks as the need built within her clit, swelling the tiny bud and leaving her hips twisting.

Tara's groan was gasoline on the fire that built within Moriko's chest. Moriko hands slid along Tara's ribs. With a whimper, Moriko tore the hard leather from Tara's chest and threw it through the door into the office. Her hands attacked the mounds she suckled on, twisting and crushing the soft flesh, driving lust in a stream from the hard brown nipples that crowned the soft breasts. Driving the desire deep into Moriko's throat and down to explode from her stomach in a fireball of need and wanting.

Tara's hands grasped Moriko's hips, her fingers slipping through the soft fur, tickling at the softness of fur and skin. Every touch sent a burst of liquid heat flowing down Moriko's mound in a ripple of flesh and

A Sample from Chasing Fae Romance Book 3: Well Met in Dragon Light

wanting. Moriko whimpered and bit her lip, her head buried between Tara's breasts as the pleasure overwhelmed her. The feel of Tara's fingers slipping over Moriko's soft mound soon had Moriko's hips shaking in need. The touch of fingers sliding along her cleft, touching, teasing but not entering soon had her whimpering into the soft pillows on Tara's chest. Moriko bit on the softness, sucking the sweet flesh deep into her mouth to cover her cries of desire as the fingers played over the soft flesh between her legs.

With a groan of her own desire bursting from her lips, Tara slid her fingers between Moriko's soft, wet lips. She slipped her fingers between the inner guardians, playing in the soft flaps, and then delving deep to release the sweet juices. Liquid flooded over Tara's palm and dribbled down Moriko's legs, burning rivers of fire on overheated nerves. Moriko's whimpers turned to screams as the pleasure exploded in repeating burst of fire along her mound. Explosions that bucked her hips and forced the invading fingers deep within Moriko's angry chasm.

Moriko's screams turned to gasps as Tara's fingers slid upwards, playing in the soft folds, dragging the hot wetness upwards. Tara's fingers played on the soft, flaps, pulling at the folds, tickling the sensitive flesh. The fingers circled Moriko's clit, pulling on the hard bud that hid beneath the soft fleshy hood. Tara's palm slapped a tattoo against Moriko's mound as fingers jerked on the hard bud between Moriko's legs. Moriko arched her back, her chin scrapping along Tara's soft chest, her eyes stared upwards at Tara staring down. Eyes met eyes and swam deeper into black depths. Mouths worked in inexpressible discourse. Their mouths slowly slid together. Moriko winced as the sensations from clit, and pussy, and nipples sliding over soft tummy flesh overwhelmed her. Moriko shuddered, a great, heaving, wracking that wiggled soft breasts and round ass.

Tara and Moriko kissed. A deep, tongue laden kiss that filled their mouths with all the need and desire that swelled between their legs. Their mouths felt swollen and full until they broke apart in an explosion of desire that left them both weak and near to collapse.

Tara was the first to recover. Her lips slipped down Moriko's chin, over her neck and down her chest. Tara stopped for a moment to suckle on the tiny breasts and the large nipples that occupied Moriko's chest. Her tongue laved over the hard crinkled flesh until they stood out, painful trees on the hillocks. Then

A Sample from Chasing Fae Romance Book 3: Well Met in Dragon Light

downward still, over the soft furry flesh of Moriko's tummy. Tara played for a moment in Moriko's navel, her tongue digging deep and teasing. Then lower still, her tongue played over Moriko's mound, and slipped, a gentle invader, along the now well-soaked cleft.

Moriko swayed in time to her screams as Tara licked along the sensitive flesh. Teased. Touched but never dived within. Never slid into that valley that Moriko wanted her to invade. Wanted with every fiber of her body. Wanted with every explosion of flame and steam between her legs. Moriko could feel her body swelling, a balloon growing between her legs. Her clit growing longer and harder with every flick of tongue on sensitive flesh until Moriko screamed wordlessly, crying for her cum, begging for the promised release.

Tara's tongue slipped into Moriko's cleft and tickled along the sensitive folds. It slipped between and deep into her cave, licking on the ridges, sucking at the sweet liquid. Moriko screamed from deep in her chest, a high-pitched whine that carried every ounce of the lust that built up in her stomach out through her larynx and up her windpipe. The light touch of Tara's tongue on her clit left Moriko screaming soundlessly, her hands gripping tightly on Tara's head. Moriko ground her pussy against Tara, pulling her into her center as if she could force that tongue even deeper into her clutching body. Moriko rolled her hips, screwing the wet probe deeper into her sensitive flesh.

Tara's tongue flicked across the hard button of Moriko's clit. Again, and again, Tara assaulted the swollen ridge of flesh. Her tongue twirled and swirled in the soft folds. Tara pushed her tongue deep into Moriko's flesh, squeezing sweet juices from the overwrought tissues. Tara fucked Moriko with her tongue, the hard wetness poking deep and then fleeing to chase the hard bud where it hid beneath its hood. Back and forth, over and over, up and then down again.

Tara hummed with joy and lust, her own need driving her. The fire twisting her mound and grinding between her legs. She could feel the swelling of her own clit as she sucked on Moriko's center. She could feel the explosions of lust and need twisting her hips and rippling up her tummy. She could feel Moriko against her forehead. Muscles that seized and then released, muscles rippling the soft mound that swelled above her. Tara's hands gripped Moriko's hips harder, trying desperately not to let the woman rip away as her pleasure built. Trying to hang on to that bud of pleasure until Moriko burst in a scream of release that rattled the

A Sample from Chasing Fae Romance Book 3: Well Met in Dragon Light

windows of the shop. Trying to push Moriko one more step closer to that heaven of complete release and relaxation.

Tara's tongue beat against the flesh of Moriko's pussy. She pushed sensation deep into the woman. She pushed lust deep into her swelling tissues until with a scream Moriko came. Moriko screamed, a high pitched squeal that burned through Tara. A high pitched scream that caused the building pressure between Tara's legs to burst in a flare of fire and ice and storm. Moriko's hips bucked as she released. Her mound smashed against Tara's nose. Her pussy ground against Tara's chin. Tara's own hips bounced and bucked. Her thighs shook as she released. Both women quivered and danced like ice cubes in a cocktail shaker. Until with a final sigh, Moriko collapsed. Her hips tore from Tara's grip and Moriko folded to lay on the ground, her chest heaving from the exertion.

Tara weaved. Her head bobbled on sapped neck muscles that could no longer spring back. Then Tara too collapsed, folding until she lay on Moriko's shoulder. Breast to breast. Nipple to nipple. Both women lay, chests heaving, legs and arms quivering.

***

Follow the continuing adventures of
Sarah, Robin, and Tara in

Chasing Fae Romance Book 1 - Well Met In Forest Light
and
Chasing Fae Romance Book 2 - Well Met in Castle Light
available now in Kindle and Paperback editions
and
Chasing Fae Romance Book 3 - Well Met in Dragon Light
coming soon in Kindle and Paperback editions

***

The Steamy Shorts series

Did you enjoy this book? Then you might enjoy the other books in the Steamy Shorts series of short story collections by Jean Ecrivain.

Welcome to the world of Jean Ecrivain's erotica short stories. Covering the range of erotica sub-genres and usually set in a world of Steampunk, Science Fiction, or Fantasy in a collection of short tales on frequently taboo subjects. The stories are hot, adult erotica and often include BDSM, menage, and alternative sexual themes. Most of the stories involve strong women who take control of their own sexuality. The stories are usually about 5,000 words long (20 pages) and include a romance story as well as the hot sex and steampunk, SF, or fantasy setting.

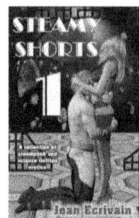

Steamy Shorts 1

Available now in Amazon Kindle and Paperback editions

In this collection of five erotic short stories for women (and their men) are:

1. The Magnificent Vibrational Relief Machine
2. Queen Bee
3. Pirate Jenny
4. Steamy Shorts
5. A Taste for the Night

Steamy Shorts 2

Available now in Amazon Kindle and Paperback editions

In this collection of five erotic short stories for women (and their men) are:

1. The Bonny Black Hare
2. The Sex Jin
3. Cyber Sexed
4. Sword and Sexery
5. Well Met in the Forest

The Steamy Shorts Series

Steamy Shorts 3

Available now in Amazon Kindle and Paperback editions

In this collection of five erotic short stories for women (and their men) are:

1. **Maids in Steam**
2. **The Egg Timer**
3. **Bad Genie**
4. **The Kinky Sex Guide**
5. **Well Met in Castle Light**

Steamy Shorts 4

Coming Soon in Amazon Kindle and Available now in Paperback editions

In this collection of five erotic short stories for women (and their men) are:

1. **Dragon Squeezes**
2. **Bad Day/Good Day**
3. **Hen Party**
4. **The Collection**
5. **Captured**

Steamy Shorts 5

Available now in Amazon Kindle and Paperback editions

In this collection of five erotic short stories for women (and their men) are:

1. The Engine Room
2. Steamy Knickers
3. Not Your Typical Ear-worm
4. The Sex Coder
5. The Barn

www.ingramcontent.com/pod-product-compliance
Lightning Source LLC
Chambersburg PA
CBHW070531281125
36049CB00033B/922